War of the Black Curtain

BOOKS IN THIS SERIES
BY JAMES DASHNER

A Door in the Woods
Book One of the Jimmy Fincher Saga

Gift of Ice
Book Two of the Jimmy Fincher Saga

The Tower of Air
Book Three of the Jimmy Fincher Saga

War of the Black Curtain
Book Four of the Jimmy Fincher Saga

BOOK FOUR
JIMMY FINCHER SAGA

War Black of the Curtain

JAMES DASHNER
ILLUSTRATED BY MICHAEL PHIPPS

SWEETWATER BOOKS
AN IMPRINT OF CEDAR FORT, INC.
SPRINGVILLE, UTAH

ISBN 13: 978-1-55517-879-6

Published by Sweetwater Books, an imprint of Cedar Fort, Inc.
2373 W. 700 S., Springville, UT 84663
Distributed by Cedar Fort, Inc., www.cedarfort.com

Cover design by Rebecca Jensen
Cover design © 2012 by Lyle Mortimer

Printed in the United States of America

10 9 8 7 6 5 4 3 2 1

Printed on acid-free paper

Dedicated to my kids.
I saved the best for last.

Acknowledgments

It seems that I thank the same people every time. But I truly mean it. My wife, Lynette, the Bahlmann family (Bob, Shirley, Zack, Brian, and Michael), Randall Spilker, Julie Wright, Judi and Angela Hansen—thanks for your time to edit and assist. Thanks for telling me not only when it was bad but also when it was good.

I'm thankful for Cedar Fort and all the hard work they put into my series. I appreciate you treating me like family.

Most of all, a big thanks to all of my readers. The past two years have been quite a trip. I've enjoyed the letters, the school visits, the signings—more than I can put into words. When I first started writing about Jimmy Fincher, patterned after a dorky kid from Georgia—me—I wouldn't have dreamed that someday other people would care a lick about it. I'm glad you do.

Contents

Prologue 1

1. Sleep 5

2. Those Pesky Dreams 10

3. Floating Lady 14

4. Rope Climbing 19

5. The Odd Present 23

6. Breakfast of Champions 28

7. Urgent Visitor 35

8. Ocean Hopping 38

9. Tanaka 41

10. The Butterflies 45

11. The Okisaru 49

12. Going on a Drive 53

13. Robed Death 59

14. Flying Car 61

CONTENTS

15. Ghost or No Ghost..65

16. The Plan Begins...71

17. Into the Mountain..74

18. Large Bedroom..77

19. Japanese Spit...80

20. Eye Shine..84

21. Beds Arise 86

22. Icy Prayer 89

23. Up the Stairs..94

24. Reunion..97

25. Bad Nickname..100

26. The Big Apple...106

27. Floating Lady's Digs...109

28. Inori 112

29. Erifani Tup...116

30. Mirror, Mirror..120

31. The Farm..127

32. Gift Number Four...132

33. Flee...136

34. Decision 138

35. Gone South 141

36. So, We Meet Again 145

37. No Deal 149

38. Gathering 153

39. A Sword of Ice..157

40. Charge..161

41. Beast of Legend 164

42. Colored Scales 167

43. Body 169

44. Knifepoint 172

45. Note from the Dead 176

46. Travel Plans 179

47. The Half 183

48. Warden of Dreams 186

49. What it Means 189

50. Raspy 193

51. The Black Coma 198

52. The Grand Exception 201

53. Into the Yumeka 205

54. Into the Stompers 206

55. Dirty Hand 209

56. Zombies 212

57. Airplane 215

58. No Parachute 219

59. Teacher 223

60. The Second Layer 228

61. Next 233

62. Mansion Again 239

63. Weird Thing in a Chair 242

64. Shadow 245

65. Piggyback 248

66. Deceived 252

CONTENTS

67. Yellow Goo..255

68. Take to the Skies 259

69. Soul Searching...263

70. In the Bag 270

71. Topsy-Turvy 274

72. Good-bye...278

Epilogue...282

About the Author...287

About the Illustrator...288

Prologue

The sound of ripping could be heard from miles away.

From the ground, the disturbance appeared to begin near a small patch of clouds, surrounded by the shadow-tainted blue of late morning. A vicious trail of black hurtled across the sky in a swath of destruction, devouring all color in its path. As a horrible tearing sound shattered the still silence of autumn, the dark line expanded, making a massive, black rent in the air. Anyone who was lucky enough to be free from the Black Coma and witness the Ripping saw it spread across the sky like a great sickness.

And then the *things* started flying out of it.

The woman sat and watched from her favorite spot atop the skyscraper. Her world had fallen into a frightening chaos. Even though she'd heard from her father over the years that it was coming, the fulfillment of such depressing foresight was still too horrible to fathom. She had always been known for her great sense of humor but saw no joke in this—the end of their lives.

Her entire city, her entire world, was falling asleep. And this was no lame attempt at philosophical discussion or metaphor. It was quite literal. The streets were full of them—prostrate, closed-eyed, breathing people. They were all in the Coma, yet very much alive.

She stood and walked back to the stairwell that led from the roof of the towering building down to her penthouse apartment. It was finally time to do something she had prepared for her whole life—ever since she'd abandoned the evil of her father.

Once inside, she went to every window and pulled the drapes closed. She turned off all of the lights. She unplugged the phones, and locked her door.

She then went into her bedroom, lay down, and closed her eyes. To many, it would look like sleep. To her, it was entering a world of madness. The Second Layer was always much worse than the First.

It was time to summon the Red Disk.

The birdcage looked like something you would pick up at any pet store, made of metal and about three feet tall. But instead of a bird, hundreds of butterflies swarmed and seethed within the cage, seeming to want nothing but to get out. Although the spaces between the bars of the cage would have allowed such an escape, the butterflies stayed within.

Their owner's name was Tanaka, and the butterflies obeyed their master, even though he smelled like some raw combination of cabbage and underarms. And he wasn't the most handsome guy to ever grace the surface of the earth. Butterflies are very forgiving. That, or they have no sense of sight or smell. Or hearing for that matter. The man's voice was enough to drive a person to have their ears removed.

He came to them in the morning, and asked for a creature to fly to him so he could show his friends the magic of the little wonders. One did, a small specimen with wings the color of the sun. It fluttered out and flew to its leader, landing softly on his hand. Then, the master spoke a command, and things changed.

A bright light flashed and descended along a straight line from the man's hand where the butterfly had rested, all the way to the ground below it like some celestial yo-yo and then disappeared. What sat there in its place made the onlookers' curiosity turn into something entirely different.

For the first time in a while, their hearts stirred with the faintest glimmer of hope.

On the other side of the planet, a man walked through the soggy fields of an abandoned farm. It was not the only spot in the world in which he currently existed, because the man could be in more than one place at the same time. *Try explaining that to any one of the billions of normal people in the world,* the man thought.

It was strange indeed, and impossible for anyone to understand except himself. But it was real and true, and a part of his life. It *was* his life—his very existence.

During his many strange and twisted years, he'd been called lots of things—most of them not very nice.

Freak.

Magician.

Alien.

Heck, one guy called him Satan once, which didn't make any sense. But to his friends, and to those who had been touched by his gift, he was known only by one name.

They called him The Half.

CHAPTER 1
Sleep

The world was falling asleep.

The pace of it seemed to be quickening, people falling over left and right, sleeping in everything from gutters to pumpkin patches. Nothing would wake them up. Not shaking. Not water. Not even the classic of all wake-up classics—pinching— would make them stir. Things were getting bad.

Which made it seem wrong that at the moment I was eating Doritos and watching *Star Wars* at my uncle's house on a big-screen TV. Seeing some gangly dude named Luke try to save the universe just wasn't as exciting as it used to be. I turned it off, got up from the couch, and headed to bed, hours after everyone else. With what was going on in the world, I was afraid of sleep.

The stairs let out their creaking whine as I shuffled up them, eerie in the silence and darkness. I got the spooks and ran the rest of the way up the steps and down the hall and into the room that I shared with my older brother, Rusty. The pale moonlight from the window revealed his face, fast asleep. Not like the Coma of the Ka—there was a definite difference: his face didn't look like a ghost's.

By habit, I reached under my bed on the other side of the room to make sure the leather carrying case holding the Red Disk was still there. It was. Trying my best to be quiet, I slipped under the covers of the bed, and laid my head down on the pillow. Rusty must not have been as asleep as I thought, because he woke up.

"For the love, Jimmy, could you be any louder? It's hard enough to sleep as it is."

"Sorry, you pansy. Next time, I won't breathe or move my covers."

Rusty yawned and rolled over to face my bed. "What've you been doing?"

"Trying to watch a movie, but I can't get my mind off things. I wonder what Tanaka and those guys are up to. They should've come back to us by now."

"They're fine, bro, quit worrying so much."

I made a disgusted face even though Rusty probably couldn't see it very well.

"Not worry? They're *fine?* Did you drink a brewsky or something? The world isn't what I would call a very safe place to be right now. All we *should* do is worry, you idiot."

"With those things Tanaka found, I'd say he's safer than us by far. Even with your *Gifts.*" He emphasized the word with unveiled sarcasm.

"Why'd you say it like that?"

Rusty pushed himself up to lean on his elbow so I could see his face. "I'm just kidding. But it's kind of lame that you can only use the Anything four times. Well, two more times, now."

I couldn't have agreed more with him. The Anything was like a cruel trick—the ability to do almost anything, the solution to all of our problems, and yet I could only use it a limited number of times. Now that I had only two more chances, it almost seemed useless because I was so scared to waste its power. Especially since Farmer, who'd given me the Third Gift, had said that I must save one of its uses for the very end.

"Well," I replied to Rusty, "I haven't heard anyone complain when the Shield or Ice have saved them, have I?"

Rusty flopped back down onto his bed. "You got me there, little bro."

We sat in silence for a while. Then Rusty surprised me when he started snoring. So much for the company.

I shifted onto my side, and looked out the window. The swaying shadows of tree branches would be my only entertainment until sleep came. So, of course, my mind drifted back to the countless problems that consumed my life.

Weeks had passed since we'd left behind the misty lands of Japan. Hood, with his magic Bender Ring, had been kind enough to take me and my family back to America. He then went with Tanaka to try and find Miyoko, Rayna, and the rest of the Alliance. With every passing day I grew more and more sick with worry about where they could be.

Everything was just plain bizarre, no doubt about it. Chaos was building even as those who remained awake tried to keep the world moving along. The latest estimates showed that roughly half the world was now in a coma, the other half trying to figure out how to avoid it. But there was no escape, I knew that now. The dark Shadow Ka were fully formed, and it would not be long before their influence conquered the rest of us. The sky was gray with their strange, lingering taint on the world.

And yet there was nothing I could do. Despite my Gifts, despite all I knew, there was nothing. Not until I discovered the secret of the Red Disk and found the Dream Warden. All of which came down to some guy or gal or monster named Erifani Tup.

Oh criminy, the thought of it all gave me a headache every time.

I shifted around and faced the wall, and finally let my eyes close. But it didn't make everything go away. It's hard to think of much else when you've been told that you're the only hope to save an entire world. Even if you don't want to be.

We hadn't seen a Shadow Ka since Japan. Our plan to go to Uncle Darin's house in South Carolina and hole up there until we could figure out what to do next seemed to have worked—even though he hadn't shown up since we'd arrived. We didn't say it, but we knew that he was probably out there, somewhere, in the Black Coma. His house was out in the country, away from the major population centers where the Ka were wreaking the most havoc. It had bought us some time—time that was now wasting away . . .

Something snapped outside the window.

My head popped off the pillow, and my ears strained to hear something more. It had sounded like someone breaking a big stick over their knee, but then it was silent.

I should look out the window, I thought. *Nah, it's probably nothing. Maybe if I hear it again . . .*

More thoughts flew through my mind. Farmer, the old Giver, whom I had not seen since receiving the Third Gift. Joseph, who was sleeping down the hall, still holding back secrets. The Stompers. They were literally our worst nightmares according to Farmer. *Now what in the heck was that supposed to mean?* So little made sense.

In the haze of my weariness, I thought I heard another sound outside. It was faint, probably just the wind . . .

Too tired to get worked up about it all over again, I finally drifted into sleep.

CHAPTER 2

Those Pesky Dreams

This time, I knew I was dreaming.

I'm clinging to a rope, thick, coarse, with climbing knots about every three feet. It reminds me of the rope in gym class, the one we were challenged to climb all the way to the top of. There had been a red bell up there, and anyone who rang it was an instant stud. I guess I was more of a slowly developing stud.

The rope is swaying just a little. My hands grip one of the knots; my feet are planted on another. I am surrounded by darkness, but for some reason I can still see my body and the rope just fine. Above me, it goes on forever, ascending to the black sky until it disappears. The same is true below. I can see no end to the rope, and no ground. I'm in the middle of nothingness, hanging on a rope.

I'm glad it's a dream.

This brings on the thought of Stompers and nightmares, giving me chills.

Not knowing what else to do, I begin to climb. Why I decide to go up instead of down is a mystery, but for some reason it makes sense. Reaching up with my left hand, I grab the next knot and pull myself up, securing my feet on the closest knot to them. Next, I reach up with my right hand, and do the process again. Left hand, right hand, pull up my feet and secure them. It's kind of fun.

I climb on. Ten minutes. Twenty minutes. Nothing is changing. Thirty minutes. My arms are tired, my hands sore from the rough rope. My feet ache from the unnatural gripping motions as I climb.

And then everything changes.

Something seemed to warp the air around me, jarring the fabric of reality for just a moment, and then I knew that I was awake. But I was not in my bed.

I clung to the rope, terrified now that the dream state seemed to have evaporated. It was impossible to explain, but I was no longer dreaming. It was . . . different. The air took on real substance, the feel of the rope no longer had a fakeness to it. It was *real.* I was hanging onto a rope in the middle of a literal nowhere.

Looking around now with a renewed desperation, I could see nothing. Darkness. Yet the rope glowed, revealing itself forever above and below me. Panic inched up my spine, and my hands began to sweat. *What is happening to me?*

I reached up and started climbing. Down seemed better now, but I had already come so far. Maybe it was all an illusion, and I would reach some magical world soon, filled with Munchkins and tin men. Arms aching, palms raw, feet cramped, I climbed.

Sweat trickled into my eyes, stinging like the dickens. I squinted, trying to squeeze out the pain. Firming my left-handed grip on the rope, I let go with my right hand and rubbed my eyes with a circling motion. It helped, and as I put my hand back onto the nearest knot, I opened my eyes.

There was a woman floating in the air before me.

It would have seemed pretty normal under usual dream conditions. Endless ropes in blackness, floating women—nothing was weird when you dreamed. But I could not get over the feeling that I was awake, and seeing the woman froze my heart for just a second.

She was very ordinary looking. Not fat, not skinny, brown hair, brown eyes, normal mom-like clothes. Her face was pleasant and kind, and for that I was glad. She didn't have wings, so her floating trick had to be magic.

"Hello, Jimmy," she said in a soft voice.

I didn't speak, not quite ready to converse with a flying woman who looked like the host of a cooking show.

"Now's not the time to be shy, young man," she continued. "I have come to give you an urgent message."

"Who are you? Why does it feel so *real* here?" I asked, giving up on the whole *don't speak* approach.

"Who am I? It doesn't matter, really. I am a messenger, just like others you have come across in your many journeys since entering the first Door. As for why it feels so lifelike and real right now, that's part of the message I've come to talk to you about." She smiled, revealing teeth that weren't quite white but nice looking all the same.

"Are you one of the Givers?"

"No."

"A member of the Alliance?"

"Um . . . sure."

"Why did you hesitate?"

"Because I am on the same team, if you will. I am on your side, Jimmy, I am on their side—the Alliance, the Givers. So . . . I guess I am one of them."

I couldn't imagine this sweet lady lying to me, so I felt better already.

"What's your message?" I asked.

"Well, I have two, and both are equally important. The first is to tell you more about things—more about the Stompers." She paused. "The second is to tell you that you must come see me. Soon."

"Come see you? Isn't that what I'm doing right now?"

"I need to see you in the . . . *real* world. I need you to bring something to me so that I can help you with it."

"What?" I asked.

She smiled again, but this time it seemed darker, more serious.

"The Red Disk."

CHAPTER 3

Floating Lady

"Wait a minute," I said. "Are you Erifani Tup?"

A look of startled curiosity crossed her face, which then turned into amusement. She reminded me of a hillbilly country singer for some reason.

"You think Erifani Tup is a person?" she asked.

"What do you mean? It's not a person?"

She waved her hand in the air as if swatting some pesky gnat. "Never mind that now. Let's speak no further of the Red Disk until you come to see me. There is much to tell you now."

From somewhere below a slight breeze began, swaying the rope and stirring the lady's hair. It seemed to bother her, and she looked down. I followed her gaze, and could see nothing of interest except the dangling, endless rope and darkness.

"What's wrong?" I asked.

"There should be no wind in this place." She looked down again. "I don't think we're as safe as I thought." Her eyes met mine, and they were full of worry, her brow creased.

"Ya know," I said, "for someone trying to clear things up

for me, you're doing one whale of a job. I'm more confused than ever, now. Why aren't we safe?"

"Okay, listen," she replied after another glance down. "I'm going to talk fast, and I want no interruptions. Got it?"

"Sure, whatever, lady. But my arms are getting awfully tired hanging on this rope."

"First," she said, ignoring my complaint, "in case we get cut off, let me tell you where to find me. I'm in a place called New York City. Have you heard of it?"

I raised my eyebrows at her, thinking she had to be kidding.

"Well, have you?" she insisted.

"Yes, I've heard of New York City. Isn't it in some weird country called America?"

Brushing off my sarcasm, she continued. "There is a building there, called the Empire State Building. You must meet me on the roof, in two days, at nine in the morning. Can you do that?"

Although it seemed very bizarre, I figured if I could go to the North Pole, I could pretty much go anywhere. But I knew Hood would have to help me, or Dad would have to drive me up there. But to keep things simple, I just nodded and filed it away in the old memory bank.

"Good," she said. The nameless floating lady then took a deep breath, paused, and started talking a mile a minute.

"The Stompers, Jimmy. You need to understand what they are because the time is coming when everything will come to a head. They are nightmares—I know you have been told this. But it is not so simple. To understand them, you must understand the nature of dreams. You must understand the Yumeka, the World of Dreams."

"The Yuma-what?" I asked.

"The *yoo-may-kah*. Yumeka. It is the place you go, where everyone goes, when they go beyond the normal dream state. It is real, as real as the skin on your body and the hair on your head. That is why it affects us so much, why we wake up sad when a dream was wonderful and we didn't want it to end, why we wake up terrified and sweating from our nightmares.

"Have you ever heard the old wives' tale that if you die in your dream, you die in real life?"

I nodded.

"It's true if you enter the Yumeka. The World of Dreams is real, Jimmy. It is a place—as much as your home in Georgia is a place, as much as Mars and the Moon are places. Sometimes when you dream, you go there."

"That seems kind of freaky," I said.

"Just hear me out. You have to realize that the Yumeka is not just a figment of your imagination. Otherwise, your mind will never accept the true nature of your enemy."

"The Stompers?"

"Yes. Their entire existence is based on the corruption of the Yumeka. After the Shadow Ka are sent into a world to initiate the Black Coma, the Stompers come in and feed off the minds of the people. They take the form of one's worst and most terrifying nightmares, and that is how they grow. Your fear is their food. And once they have you, there is no escape, no waking. Except for the Grand Exception."

"What's that?"

"The Grand Exception. The one rule they cannot resist, the ultimate sacrifice."

"And what is it?" I asked. Her words were confusing and fascinating at the same time. I felt like a fingerless boy at a nose-picking convention.

"A person can voluntarily take the place of another who is in the clutches of the Stompers. And they must accept—it is a rule of the universe, unbreakable. Unfortunately, they usually don't have to worry about it because their ultimate goal is to have everyone in their grasp anyway. Everyone."

She jogged my memory. "The Givers called it 'dying' for someone else, I think. One of them did it for Joseph when he was taken away by the Ka."

"Yes, you're right," she said. "And the word works in more ways than you know. To be in the control of the Stompers is worse than death, if anything is. There is no escape. There is no hope. Even the Grand Exception is so remote, and in the end, so useless, because they will probably just get you later anyway."

Her eyes filled with tears, and her next words shook with emotion.

"Oh, Jimmy, you sweet, brave boy. It is a terrible thing, your future. I shake with fear when I think of what you face in the days ahead. The Fourth Gift will put a burden on you the likes of which no one has ever known."

"The Fourth Gift? You know what it is?"

"Soon, Jimmy, soon. But you must come to me later for that. We're not done here yet." She rubbed her eyes, and I expected her to plummet without the use of her hands to hold herself up. Then I remembered she was just floating. *I live a strange life,* I thought.

"I need to tell you about the Layers of the Yumeka. This will perhaps be the most shocking news of all, the most disturbing."

"What is it?"

"The Stompers take their victims through endless loops,

or cycles, of dreams. Their evil hunger for fear is best fed in the beginning stages of nightmares, before the dreamer becomes immune to it. They manipulate your mind so they can essentially erase your memories after a time, and then start from scratch. They take you fresh and happy into a new nightmare, enjoying and feeding off of your innocent and raw fear. When you become immune to that one, they erase your memories again, and begin anew. Over and over, for as long as they can keep your body alive, they take you from one nightmare to the next, starting from scratch each time. They're called Layers."

If I was confused before, now my mind was ready to give up. It was like some guy in a tight red jumper from a bad *Star Trek* episode had just set his phaser to "stun" and fired it on my brain. And the lady wasn't about to let up and offer time for questions.

"Now, Jimmy, about these Layers. I know it's confusing, but we . . ."

A gust of wind rushed upward, much faster than the one before. Floating Lady quit talking and gasped, as if the wind carried tiny needles that dug into her flesh. She looked at me, her face a mask of concern. Her next words made my spine do its own version of the jimmy-legs.

"We've run out of time."

The wind picked up, roaring from below like the breath of some giant beast.

Which, come to find out, was exactly correct. Kind of.

CHAPTER 4

Rope Climbing

The lady's hair flapped in all directions as she looked around her. It didn't take a rocket scientist to figure out something terrible was happening. Her face was pale with fright.

"What's going on?" I asked, speaking up over the increasing sound of rushing wind.

"You have to go, quickly!" she yelled. "You have seen this before—it's the Wall of the Stompers. If they get you before the Fourth Gift, it may all be wasted! Climb!"

"Climb? Where to? There's nothing up there!"

"It's not *literally* up there! Your mind, Jimmy, your thoughts! Just climb, and escape!"

As I tried to sort out her words, the wind picked up even faster and changed directions without warning, coming from above, pushing me down toward the abyss below. Thoughts and memories popped into my head—terrible ones of the Door in the woods, on the lake, in the desert with Farmer . . . .

I knew what was coming before I saw it. And so I began to climb.

"Hurry!" the lady screamed in my ear, floating upward with me.

"Well, why don't you help for Pete's sake?" I yelled back at her.

"I can't," she said with sadness in her voice, barely audible over the sucking wind. "I must go now. Climb, boy, and be safe! I will see you in two days!"

And then she was gone, her image flashing away like a turned-off TV.

"Wait!" I screamed, even though I knew it was useless.

Knowing it would only make things worse, I looked down anyway. Far below, the rope was being swallowed by a rising floor of blackness, somehow darker than what it had looked like before. I had seen this wall too many times already in my life, and knew that nothing good could come of letting it catch up to me.

I looked back up and started climbing all over again. My arms ached and felt rubbery as I pulled myself up, knot by knot. Above, the glowing rope extended for as far as I could see. The Floating Lady's words about it all being in my head came to mind but didn't help. The wind got faster and faster, making the arduous climb even harder. There was no way I could keep it up much longer.

I paused and looked down again. My heart slipped around inside my chest when I saw that the rising wall of blackness was already halfway closer than last time I'd taken a peek. I could see it now—it's writhing, sucking sea of goo coming for me. The lady had called it the Wall of the Stompers. Was that what they . . . looked like? I couldn't conceive of our bitter enemy looking like tar.

Whatever it was, it wanted me inside of it.

Shaking off my thoughts, I climbed. My body ached, sweat was making my hands slippery, and the wind tore at my clothes and hair, but I climbed. As I grabbed and pulled at each knot, a panic filled me that I hadn't felt in some time. Who knew if my Gifts worked here? This place could have totally different rules.

Nothing was coming into view above. I was going nowhere, and my arms and legs burned, begging me to quit. Again, I stopped and looked down. The Wall was only a hundred yards below me, rising with a vengeance. Trying my best to calm my nerves, I threw my thoughts into the Ice, sending a blast of cold chunks with all the force I could manage into the oncoming Wall.

The Ice struck it, shattering its flat surface, like an overweight uncle doing a cannonball into the pool. Great spouts of the goo shot up from all sides of where the Ice had struck and then came together and swallowed the Ice until it disappeared. The blackness shifted and settled back into a flat shape, and continued upward, not missing a beat.

It was now fifty yards below me.

I climbed up a few more knots, and knew it was over. I couldn't do it anymore—my limbs were spent. The Wall of the Stompers was now thirty yards below. I gripped the rope, closing my eyes, thinking. *What did she mean, what did she mean? It's my mind, my thoughts. Think!*

I looked again. Ten yards away. With a scream, I threw everything within my soul into the Ice, blasting the world below me. The Wall flashed as a sheet of thick Ice slammed into it, repelling it forty or fifty yards downward. The black goo cracked through, burying any remnants of the cold stuff, and began to climb again.

It came quicker, as if it were angry now. Again, I slammed it with all the strength of my Second Gift. The Ice repelled it again, throwing it down another forty or fifty yards. But in seconds the blackness overcame it, and rose again. I couldn't keep it down forever. Between the climbing and the mental energy of using the Gift, I was barely able to hold onto the rope.

Forty yards away. Thirty yards. Twenty.

My mind worked like crazy, trying to think up a solution. *My thoughts, my mind.*

I thought of the bed. I had been sleeping in the bed at my uncle's house when all of this began. Nothing seemed like I was dreaming anymore, but it had to be. Dreams had taken on a new meaning now, but still . . .

The bed. Surely my body was still in that bed. *The bed.* I concentrated my mind on that one thing, focused all my thoughts on it. *The bed.*

The Wall was almost on me, the force of its sucking wind ripping at my body. I could see its shaking, evil goo reaching for me. When it was five feet below, I was ready. Without looking above, I held onto my thought, and reached for what I wanted.

The world shimmered, and *I am suddenly dreaming again. Everything is different.*

The Wall of goo reaches my feet, repelled by the Shield. The Wall swells as it rises up and around the protective force, fully encasing me in a bubble of blackness. Soon it cuts off both ends of the rope, and the faint glow disappears, leaving me in complete darkness. The air grows stale and reeks of dank, rotting leaves. I close my eyes, take a deep breath.

And then I wake myself up.

CHAPTER 5

The Odd Present

Rusty was screaming at me.

"Jimmy, wake up! WAKE UP!"

He shook my shoulders and slapped my face.

"I'm up!" I yelled, my cheek stinging. "I'm up, you idiot! Get off!"

Rusty shrank back, and sat down on his bed. He was sweating, and looked scared out of his wits.

"What's wrong with you?" I asked.

"You were going nuts, man! I thought you were falling into the Coma."

I rubbed my eyes with both hands and tried to shake off the absolute reality of the dream I'd just had. I knew my life was strange, but this was almost too much.

"Oh, man, this is weird," I said. "Maybe I was . . . I don't know. I just had the craziest dream."

Rusty was still breathing heavily but started to calm down a bit. "What was it?" he asked.

"It was whacked-out. It's hard to explain, but I was dreaming, and then something happened to me . . . . I wasn't

23

dreaming anymore but still in the place of the dream. And then later I switched back again, right before I woke up."

"Whacked-out? I'd say so," Rusty said.

"I'm dead serious. This lady came to me like some angel and told me all this stuff about the Stompers. And about dreams—the World of Dreams—how they're actually real and all this weird stuff. She said I was supposed to come visit her."

"Visit her? Where?"

"New York City." My face blushed as if I were telling a doctor that I'd been seeing talking bunnies in the shower. "The Empire State Building of all places."

Rusty looked at me with his mouth open, playing his role as the doctor who'd been told about the bunnies. I waited for his diagnosis of insanity.

"Jimmy, I don't doubt anything anymore. We better go talk to Mom and Dad."

"It's still the middle of the night. Let's just wait until the morning."

"You really think you can go back to sleep?"

"I . . ."

There was a loud crash outside. Rusty and I jumped up and ran to the window. It had sounded like someone falling into the bushes, twigs snapping and leaves shaking. Rusty pushed up the window, grunting with the effort—it was old and heavy. We both popped our heads out at the same time and looked down. The moonlight coming through the taint of the Ka painted a dead, silver glow over everything, and we could see the place where the bushes had been messed up. Something caught my attention to the right, a shadow disappearing around the corner of the house.

"There!" I yelled. "Did you see that?"

"What?"

"I saw someone running away, around the house. Come on!"

I pulled my head back in the window and ran out of the room. Rusty followed right behind. We flew down the creaky stairs and ran to the front door, not wasting time on shoes. Seconds later we were walking around the yard barefoot, searching everywhere for signs of the intruder. We found no traces a person had ever been there, except for the broken bush. It was easy to figure out that whoever it was had been trying to climb up to our window and had slipped and fallen.

"Who in the world could it have been?" Rusty asked.

"I don't have a clue." The cool air of the night made me shiver. I took in a deep breath and felt the crispness of fall. In better times, it would've gotten me excited for football and Halloween. "Should we keep searching, walk down the road a bit?"

"I don't know. I'm too creeped out. Let's go wake up Dad."

"Okay, come on."

We were walking toward the front door when Rusty pulled up, stood still. He was staring at a spot in the yard about twenty feet away, under a small tree.

"What?" I asked.

"I think our spy left something for you."

I ran to the tree and knelt down to get a good look at the object. I couldn't believe it. Rusty ran up behind me and picked the thing up. He turned it over in his hands, disbelief in his eyes as well.

"Are you sure you didn't leave this here?" he asked.

"Are you kidding? I haven't seen one of those in a long time, and even if I did have one, I wouldn't leave it out here."

"Just when I think it couldn't get any stranger . . . come on."

We ran into the house and up to the room Mom and Dad were sleeping in. Dad was fully recovered now from his near-miss Shadow Ka experience, although it had been a difficult healing process. His body had been through some downright unnatural mutations—growing wings on your back made for more than just a little itchy skin. The thought of how close we came to losing him to those monsters still made my skin crawl. It had been too close for comfort.

"What's going on?" he asked in a groggy voice after I shook him awake. Rusty went around the bed and woke up Mom, and then sat next to her.

"Are you guys okay?" she asked.

"Yeah," I said. "It's just been a weird night. I had a crazy dream, and then we saw someone running away from the house after they tried to spy on us."

"What!" Mom shot to a sitting position, worry spreading across her face like clouds over a lake.

"Mom, everything's fine," I said, wishing there was a better way to tell everything to everybody. "Just hear us out, I think we're fine. It wasn't a Shadow Ka, and they left something. A sign, I think. Maybe it was to show us they're on our side."

"If they're on our side," Rusty asked, "why are they trying to climb up the house to peek in our window while we're asleep?"

"WHAT!" Mom asked again, this time even louder.

"Mom, Mom, calm down."

Dad finally spoke up. "What did they leave behind?"

Rusty handed it to Dad, who then turned it over and over in his hands, trying to see it better in the faint light coming from the hallway.

"What is it?" Mom asked.

"It's a . . . Braves hat," he said and then looked at her and held it up.

"Yeah," I answered. "And I'm positive it's the one I lost at that lake in Utah."

CHAPTER 6
Breakfast of Champions

It was the mark on the inside sweatband of the hat that gave it away. I'd put my initials there with a blue pen, and there was no mistaking the handwriting or the smudged letters, "J. F." The water from the lake had crinkled and yellowed the hat itself, but I had no doubt that it was mine.

"That's just plain bizarre," Mom said after I explained it to them.

"I know," I said. "But I've been thinking about it, and I think it means there was someone there that day, or soon after, watching out for me or something."

"Or maybe it was that hairy dude, Dontae," said Rusty. "He could've gone to get it before he went back into the Blackness."

"I'd have to agree, son," said Dad. "If someone was there looking out for you, they sure didn't offer much help." I remembered that awful day, when Dad had shown up to save me right before the boat disappeared into the Blackness.

"Maybe whoever it was got there too late or something, I don't know. But why would Hairy, or Dontae, or whatever that pig is called, take time to find the hat? I can't imagine it was him."

"Well," said Mom, "whoever it was, I'm sure they'll be back, so we better keep our eyes open. I guess our little secret hiding place is no longer such a secret."

"Jimmy," said Dad, "what were you talking about when you said you had a weird dream?"

"It's a long story, so maybe we should wake up Joseph too."

Dad thought for a second. "No, let's save it for the morning. We all need to get some sleep—especially if you've been up for a while."

Although I couldn't imagine being able to sleep, I agreed, and went with Rusty back to our room. We talked for a while about everything, until exhaustion overcame my whirlwind thoughts, and I soon fell back into dreams.

The next morning, I sat at my uncle's kitchen table with Joseph and my whole family. Dad whipped up his famous eggs and cheese grits, with sausage and toast, and we were soon all eating like kings. But everyone was silent for the most part, deep in thought over the latest developments.

I'd taken my fourth bite of grits when Joseph couldn't stand it anymore.

"Would you people quit jamming food down your throats for one minute and tell me what in the heck happened last night? You're all acting like someone lined your undies with sandpaper."

Rusty laughed, spitting a small piece of egg onto my plate.

"Oh, thanks, Rusty," I said. "I guess I'm done." I pushed

my plate aside and looked over at Joseph. His bald head and angular face had a huge smile on it; he was tickled to death that my breakfast had been ruined.

"Joseph," I said, "I know you wear some strange clothes during the day, but do you have to wear pajamas that are even worse?" He was wearing a green tank top with red- and white-striped flannel pants, and no socks on the two monstrosities he called feet.

"Show me some love, Jimmy," he said. "I'm your best buddy on this planet. Now let's say you give me a nice foot massage while you tell me about last night?"

He thumped his white, bony, gnarled foot up next to me on the table, and something deep in my stomach begged for mercy.

"Ah, no thanks." I said. "I'd rather give Tanaka a sponge bath than ever touch those feet of yours."

Joseph laughed out loud and slapped me on the back. "Boy, it's good to see you still joking after all this. Now shut up and tell me about last night."

"How can I shut up *and* tell you?" I asked.

He wiped the grin off of his face and raised his eyebrow, not saying a word.

"All right, all right," I said.

I spent the next twenty minutes telling them everything. The sound I heard outside, the dream, the Floating Lady, her description of the dream world called the Yumeka and how the Stompers worked. I told them about the Wall of the Stompers rising from below, sucking in everything just like it had the other times I'd seen it. I told them about how my mind pulled me out of it. Then I let Rusty take over and tell the story of how we heard the crash in the bushes and everything after that.

When he was done, no one said a word. A couple of minutes went by in silence.

"A *Braves* hat?" Joseph asked.

"Yeah, a Braves hat," I said. "But I hardly think that was the most interesting part of the story, Joseph. What about the Yumeka and all that stuff about the Stompers?"

"Oh, I already knew all that."

"What?" I asked, standing up. "You know what she's talking about?"

"Of course I do."

"Well, why haven't you told us anything?"

"Jimmy, sit down," he said. I slowly sank back into my chair, angry at Joseph for the first time since we'd met.

"Listen to me," he continued. "Don't look at me like that. You know me. You know I would have told you if I could, if I thought by doing so it would have helped." He let out a huge sigh. "When the little girl, the little Giver girl—when she saved me, and when the rest of the Givers banded together to send me through the Black Curtain back to you guys, they made me promise not to tell you anything. They said it had to be revealed in its own due time or you wouldn't be able to handle it. So, I've kept my mouth shut."

I leaned back in my chair, staring at him. My anger faded, and I knew he was telling the truth.

"Can you help us understand it, now?" I asked.

"Yeah—I can't tell you everything, but I can tell you a lot."

When he didn't continue, I said, "Well?"

"That lady was right about everything. The Stompers are literally nightmares, and their venue is the Yumeka—where they trap you and hold onto you for as long as your body lives, cycling you over and over through terrifying dreams. Our fear is what feeds them, what makes them thrive and grow. It's horrible, guys. Remember, I've been in their grasp."

The thought of Joseph being snatched up by the Shadow Ka filled my mind, and the horror of that moment came back in full force. We found out later that he'd been taken to a huge structure that looked like his face made out of the black goo, and was flown into its eye. Somehow, that face represented entering the realm of the Stompers. He had only escaped because the Giver—the little girl—had sacrificed herself and taken his place.

Then it hit me. "The Grand Exception," I whispered, realizing I'd forgotten to tell them about that part.

"Yes," Joseph replied. "That was what saved me. The Grand Exception."

"Now what're you talking about?" asked Rusty.

"It's some universal law that even the Stompers can't fight against," said Joseph. "If someone is willing to take your place in their clutches, they have to let it happen. They have to switch. That's what saved me."

"It's what she meant by telling us she would die for him," I said. Everyone looked at me. "But Farmer told me it was just the best way of expressing how permanent and awful it is. I don't think she's really dead—just lost in the Yumeka, captive in their world of nightmares."

"This is how it works," said Joseph. "The Shadow Ka's purpose is twofold. They are the ones who scare us into the Coma with some kind of mind-controlling power. Then, we enter the Yumeka, and another Ka there takes us to the Stompers, symbolized to us by being flown into the eye of our own face—the face made out of that black gooey stuff. Once inside, our minds are forever trapped—captives of the

Stompers, where nightmare after nightmare will keep us in a state of terror. The Shadow Ka make sure our bodies are fed and nourished while we sleep in the Coma, keeping us alive for as long as possible.

"But then it gets worse. After a time, we become immune to it, and our minds begin to shut down. To prevent that, the Stompers put us into what they call another Layer, where our memories are altered and we're put back into a nice, wonderful world where it can start all over again. The Shadow Ka pretend to come again, we fall asleep, and we're taken back to the Stompers. This goes on in a vicious cycle forever."

"I don't understand the whole Layer thing," I said. "That's making my mind spin."

"Well, it should . . ."

Joseph was cut off by an odd humming noise in the next room. It sounded like a swarm of bees, loud and menacing. As one, we all stood up and ran to where the sound was coming from.

It only took me a second to realize what was happening, and it definitely had nothing to do with bees.

CHAPTER 7

Urgent Visitor

In the center of the living room, near the ceiling, a red circle appeared, emitting a soft glow. It looked like a magical hula hoop suspended in the air, and by now, we all knew that description wasn't very far off. The ring sunk to the ground at a fast pace, and in its path, as it lowered, the image of a man appeared. Below the ring, there was nothing but air. Above the ring, there was the man. This went on until the red circle finally touched the ground, and a very large, very robed, very hooded man was standing in front of us.

The red circle was called the Bender Ring. The robed man was one of my very best friends, even though he spoke with his finger.

The Hooded One was back.

I ran up and gave him a big hug. Hood hated when people got near him, but I didn't care. He shrunk away and didn't return the embrace, but at least he didn't push me away like usual. His burlap-looking robe scratched my skin. The droopy hood that concealed his face shook as he bent over to pick up the Bender Ring. He leaned against it, and then walked his way over to the stone fireplace.

"So what happened?" I asked. "Where's Tanaka? Did you guys find Rayna and Miyoko?" I'd been so worried about our friends of the Alliance, I couldn't stand having to wait for Hood's slow replies.

His pale white hand slipped into view from the folds of his robe, and he held it up, motioning for me to shut up and be patient. He bent down, and started painting words on the bricks with his finger. I'd gotten used to his bizarre gift and unique way of communicating, but I wasn't sure how my uncle would feel about having white paint all over his nice fireplace.

"I BRING BAD NEWS," he painted in his usual messy handwriting.

My stomach did a backward flip. Mom let out a little whimper and Rusty mumbled something under his breath that I couldn't understand.

"What is it?" Joseph asked.

Hood's draped head shook back and forth, his usual attempt to convey his uneasiness. Something was very wrong.

"THERE IS NO TIME. WE MUST HURRY."

"Hood, what are you talking about?" I said, frustrated. "Are they okay? Where are they?"

"NO TIME!!!!!" he wrote, adding several exclamation marks. "WE MUST GO—NOW."

"Go where?"

"RAYNA AND MIYOKO ARE CAPTURED." He shifted to a new spot free of white paint. "JIMMY, YOU MUST GO BACK WITH ME."

"Where?" I asked again.

"THE CAVES OF MOUNT FUJI."

"Caves of . . . what are they doing there?" Dad asked.

"I TOLD YOU. THEY ARE CAPTURED. I NEED JIMMY'S HELP!"

"Who has them, Hood?" I asked.

"WHO DO YOU THINK?"

"The Shadow Ka."

"NO, MUCH WORSE."

He stood up, paced a few steps away, and then came back again, shaking his head the entire time. Both of his white hands flashed out and he made fists to the sky. Then, taking us by surprise, he walked over to the nearest wall. With a silent rush of rage he used his right arm to swipe several framed pictures off of the wall, all of them crashing to the ground with the sound of breaking glass. We all stared, shell-shocked to see him so upset.

"Who has them?" I asked again.

Hood looked over at me through his robe. Then, caring nothing for my uncle's wall, he wrote his next phrase in huge, sprawling letters across several feet where the pictures had been.

"SOON THE STOMPERS WILL."

CHAPTER 8

Ocean Hopping

The sight of those words, although not really a surprise, affected me more than I would've thought. Knowing a little now about what it was like to be captured by the Stompers, on top of having it happen to people we cared so much about, made it seem so real, and so terrible. I sank to the floor of the room and stared at Hood, not knowing what to say.

Mom was crying, like usual. Dad and Joseph were staring into space, their faces unreadable. Rusty had his back to me, shaking his head. After a moment of complete silence, Hood wrote more words on the wall.

"TANAKA IS WAITING FOR US. WE MUST GO."

I knew he was right. Of all the people in the world, I was the one most capable of helping rescue Rayna and Miyoko, and the other members of the Alliance if they'd found them. But my heart was sick, and it had been a long time since I'd felt so much despair. I just wanted to be done with it—done with all the nonsense that I was the one destined to save everyone. I was flat-out sick of that burden.

But sometimes in life, when deep down we know we have

no choice but to move forward and take the only action that is right, we just do it. I stood up and rubbed my eyes.

"Okay, Hood. Let's go."

Even Mom didn't complain. She usually put forth at least a token resistance when I set off to save the world, but this time she stayed quiet, knowing that it had to be. *Good grief,* I thought, *this time last year I was picking my nose and watching football.*

"You come right back here when you find them," Dad said. "In fact, maybe I should go too."

"No, no, no," said Joseph. "Someone needs to stay here and look out for everyone. You stay here, J.M., and I'll go with these knuckleheads."

"No, I'll go," said Rusty.

I held my hands up. "Listen, you guys. Just stay here, all right? I can't waste time trying to let everyone hold onto me so they have the Shield. At least I have that, Tanaka has his . . . creatures, and Hood here is like some magical wizard or something—he always seems to survive. Just stay."

"He's right," Mom said. No one liked it, but that was that.

"Okay," I said. "In two days I have to meet that lady in New York. Supposedly she's going to help me figure out the riddle of the Red Disk and find the Dream Warden. So Hood will have to help me get there. If we're lucky, we can get everyone back here before then. But if we can't, I'll go straight there, and try to get you a message."

"What in the heck do we do if the Ka come knocking at our door?" asked Rusty. "Or what about our little intruder last night?"

"I don't know," I said, a little annoyed. "I would guess you'll be better off than going into a cave full of who knows what. Make do."

Not waiting for his answer, I ran upstairs to get the small leather carrying case we'd found to keep the Red Disk safe. It had a long strap that I could pull over my arm and wrap around the other side of my neck. It looked dangerously similar to a purse, but I was willing to risk my manliness to make sure I didn't lose the stupid thing. I ran back down to the living room.

"I'll take this just in case I don't make it back here," I said, motioning to the leather case. "Well, let's get going."

I gave everyone a hug and then told Hood I was ready. He moved me over to the spot in the middle of the room where he'd dropped the Bender Ring. I stood as close to him as I could, and he lifted the Ring up over our heads.

"Rusty, look after Mom and Dad for me, okay?" I said, trying to make a joke. He nodded, and did his best to smile, letting me know that everything was cool between us.

"Be careful, Jimmy," Mom said.

"I will."

Joseph started to say something smart-alecky, but I never heard him finish.

Hood brought down the Ring, and seconds later I was back in Japan.

CHAPTER 9

Tanaka

The Ring had barely hit the ground when two stinky arms wrapped around my neck and chest, and I heard the animal-like guffaw of Tanaka. He sounded like a hyena pumped up on Mountain Dew. His rotten breath washed over me as he laughed and squealed with delight to see me.

I returned the hug, just as glad to see him. His greasy hair and long eyebrows were a welcome sight. But things humbled quickly when we both remembered why I had come in the first place.

"Jimmy-san," he said in his high, deranged voice. "We live in hard times, *neh?*"

"Yeah, Tanaka, I guess we do."

A look of grief came over his face, something so rare that it took me aback. But it made perfect sense. His own daughter was trapped in a living nightmare.

I looked around and took in my surroundings. It was nighttime, and we stood on a sidewalk in the middle of a huge city. There weren't many people around, but bright neon signs shone from everywhere, with those funky Japanese letters written all over them. The air was moist and cold, like it had just rained. Typical smells of the city made my nose cringe—gas, trash, air pollution. Or maybe it was just Tanaka, it was always hard to tell.

"Where are we?" I asked.

"Ah, Jimmy-san, we in fun place, my friend. This called Tokyo! You know?"

After all I'd been through, I pretty much felt like an adult. But people must've still thought I was an idiot kid because now I'd been asked if I had heard of New York City and Tokyo within the last several hours.

"Yeah, Tanaka, I'm not as dumb as you look."

He didn't get my joke, and slapped me on the back.

"Come on, my friends," he said, grabbing Hood's and my arms.

"We go to mountain first thing tomorrow."

I wasn't very prepared for what we saw as Tanaka took us through the streets of downtown Tokyo. Everywhere we looked, people were lying on the sidewalks and in the streets, deep in the Coma of the Stompers. Most shops and businesses were closed, and it wasn't just because of the late hour. Every once in a while we saw a police car or fire truck, but for the most part, it looked as if there weren't enough people awake to help those who weren't.

The world was in bad shape.

"Have you seen any Ka around here lately?" I asked as we walked down a long and dark alley. The click of Hood's Ring as he moved along using it as a cane echoed up the damp walls of the tall buildings.

"Here and there," said Tanaka. "But I avoid them good. They no like my smell, *neh?*"

"Imagine that," I said.

Just then, a faint shadow crossed our path, and I looked to the sky on instinct. I caught the tail end of a winged beast as it disappeared above a building.

"Jeez, I just saw one up there!"

Tanaka paused to look up and then motioned to a side door, old and dilapidated.

"Come, quick. He probably not notice us so far up. In here."

He took out a key and opened the door. It squeaked on rusty hinges as it swung wide, and the three of us entered. The place was small and dank, and smelled like a locker room. Tanaka flipped a switch, and a single light bulb turned on, hanging from the ceiling with no cover. It was a one-room apartment, with no furniture except a table and two metal chairs. A small stove and kitchen took up one corner.

"How did you get this place?" I asked.

"Found a man sleeping out there." He pointed to the door. "Stole his key and tried every door until one open. Genius, *neh?*"

"More like thief, *neh?*" I replied.

"Ah, no worry. He wake up, we move out. Sit, sit!"

Hood wasted no time and snagged one of the two chairs, setting his Bender Ring on the table. Tanaka grabbed my arm and made me sit in the other. He walked over to a small closet, opened its door, and pulled out a large object.

It was the birdcage. And the butterflies were all inside, flying around like windblown leaves.

"Remember my friends?" Tanaka asked.

How could anyone ever forget? I wondered. The memory of that day came rushing back.

The day Tanaka introduced us to his purpose in life.

CHAPTER 10
The Butterflies

It had been the day after he showed up at the hotel—we hadn't seen him since he jumped off of our yacht in the middle of the ocean. I would never forget the look on Miyoko's face after she watched her own father disappear into the cold, black water. It was like mine must've looked when I realized my dad was turning into a Shadow Ka.

But soon after, she'd told me that there had to be something behind it, some reason, because her dad was not crazy. Tanaka had proven her right.

He showed up the night I'd saved my dad from the Blackness, carrying the same birdcage he'd just pulled out of the closet, full of the same butterflies, their bright colors fluttering about like living artwork. We'd been shocked, of course, at seeing him, and the cage full of pretty bugs had just made it all the more strange.

We were able to put the little things aside a bit that night as we had our grand reunion with Tanaka. As we hugged and caught him up on what we'd been through, I couldn't help but feel sick that Miyoko wasn't there to see her dad safe and sound. But she and Rayna had already set off to try and find the rest of the Alliance.

After a few minutes, he told us that he was exhausted and had to rest. We were eager to hear his story but swallowed our impatience and let the stinky man sleep. He did—for twenty-four hours straight, driving us insane with curiosity. The next evening, he didn't tell us everything, but what he showed us left me speechless, and I still had a hard time accepting it weeks later.

How he swam through the ocean and made it to land was a mystery even to him, and hard to swallow for us, but he insisted it was true. He said that an image entered his mind, a seed left by the huge monkey—the one we'd seen in the woods—that sprouted into a full-fledged vision in his head. He knew, without any doubt, that he had to dive into the ocean. When he did, he said that everything went dark, and he fell asleep. Hours later he woke up and was lying on a beach in Japan.

Dazed, confused, but still aware of the message that had burst forth in his head, he went to the place he knew he had to, deep in a forest nearby. When he got there, something was waiting for him, something that he claimed was the entire purpose of his existence.

He stopped at this point in his story, and all of us berated him, insisting he continue telling us what happened.

"No, my friends," he had said. "Let me show you."

He turned toward the birdcage, and called out a command in Japanese.

"*Kure!*"

One single butterfly, bright yellow, slipped through the bars of the cage and flew over to Tanaka, landing on his hand.

"Jimmy-san," he said. "Keep your eyes pulled, *neh?*"

"I think you mean *peeled*," I said, wondering what in the heck he was about to do.

"Yeah, yeah, that what I mean." He smiled at me and then turned his attention to the small specimen in his hand. Its wings were still fluttering, but it rested in the middle of Tanaka's palm.

"*Tskure*," he whispered.

A bright light flashed in his palm, seeming to devour the butterfly in a burst of flame. Tanaka drew his hand back, and the light floated in the air. Then it expanded into a stream of bright fluorescence, dropping toward the ground, until a band of light stood before us, like the string of a fully extended, flaming yo-yo, blinding in its brilliance. Then, with no warning or sound, the light disappeared.

Sitting there, having appeared from nowhere, was a very large monkey.

"Say hello, my good friends," said Tanaka. He pointed to the animal. "Say hello to the *okisaru*."

Rusty, taking Tanaka a tad more literally than he intended, said, "Hello."

As for me, I could only stare. It seemed years ago when we had been on the mountainside near the Pointing Finger, looking for Hood, and bumped into the huge monkey. Tanaka had told us that it was a beast of legend—the *okisaru*—that was supposed to be wise beyond imagination, and very powerful. At the time, the monkey touched Tanaka's head, hypnotizing him or something, and then disappeared into the forest.

And there he was again, sitting before us. And just to top it off, just in case we were getting too used to weird things, he had turned from a butterfly *into* a monkey.

Tanaka was beaming, looking between his pet and us, smiling like there was nothing wrong in the world.

"Uh, Tanaka," I said, "could you maybe explain a few things to us?"

"Explain?" he said. "What need to explain?" He pointed to the monkey. "This is an *okisaru*. All of my creatures are *okisaru*. They have devoted their existence to serving me." He walked over and put his arm on my shoulder. "To serve me, so that I can serve you. We are here, we are your army."

"Huh? You and a bunch of butterflies that can turn into monkeys? What's that gonna do against the Stompers?"

Tanaka shook his head, and frowned. "You make Uncle Tanaka very sad. Have some faith, *neh*?" He snapped his fingers and clapped his hands a couple of times.

And then things got really weird.

CHAPTER 11

The Okisaru

The butterflies swarmed out of the cage. Colors flashed as they expanded into a huge mass of writhing wings and antennae, filling the room all around us. Red and blue and yellow and green and black and brown, flying around and above us. I felt like I was in a huge paint mixer.

Tanaka laughed. "Jimmy-san, open the door."

"What? Why?"

"Open the door, boy! This room way too small!"

I walked over with careful steps, scared I would squash a butterfly, and opened the door into the night. Without hesitation, the swarm of bugs flew past me into the streets. They seemed to glow, filling the place with light where before there had only been darkness. Tanaka was at my ear as I looked on in wonder.

"What you want them to be?" he whispered.

I turned to look at him. "Huh? What do you mean?"

"You quit asking dumb questions, *neh*? I say, what do you want them to be? You speak English—always make fun of Tanaka's English, *neh*? Answer my question."

"What do I want them to be? You mean . . ."

Tanaka nodded his head. "Yes, Jimmy-san, like your fancy Gift. Anything."

It seemed way too crazy to be true, but then again, I had sworn a long time ago to never doubt again.

"I . . . I want them to be . . . tigers."

Tanaka yelled out an odd guttural roar.

The butterflies organized themselves at once, as if they all shared the same brain. They flew to the ground and landed in several straight rows, about three feet apart, forming a grid of colored dots filling the entire street.

A bright light flashed where each butterfly rested, a blinding sea of radiance that made me cover my eyes. I squinted and peeked through my fingers because I didn't want to miss what happened next. In perfect unison, the lights floated upward, leaving a line of fluorescence connecting it to the ground. When they had reached three feet or so, the band of lights flared a moment then disappeared. My eyes had to readjust a bit, and then I saw that Tanaka had not been exaggerating.

There were orange- and black-striped tigers everywhere.

They looked very mean—four feet tall, six feet long, and muscles rippling through their colored fur with every move. Several of them revealed their sharp teeth as they yawned and let out a small roar.

"Will they hurt us?" I asked.

"Hurt us?" asked Tanaka. "You crazy? The *okisaru* on our side, only obey me. No matter what shape they take. And they understand every word we say. Very smart, these guys."

I couldn't take my eyes off of them. There had to be hundreds, packed into the street and beyond. They seemed so out of place in the city.

"What . . . *are* they?" I asked.

"Ah, yes," he said, his voice very contemplative. "They are many things. Changelings, I have heard them called. Magical creatures. I only know them as the *okisaru*."

"Didn't Miyoko say that means big monkey?"

"Yes, yes. For some reason, that is their favorite shape. But make it very hard to get them around!" He laughed, a loud bark that actually startled some of the tigers. He yelled out a new command, and they turned back into the butterflies, bright lights and all.

"Wow. It's just unbelievable. How did you survive the ocean? What did that monkey do to your brain when he touched you? How in the world did all this come about?"

"Ah, Jimmy-san, you leave that to me, *neh*? Just know this." He held up the birdcage for the butterflies to fly back into. "The *okisaru* are your army, and I am their general. We help you win this war."

"Well . . . thanks. I could use the help."

That had been weeks ago, and the memory of it still made me shake my head. Now, sitting there with Hood and Tanaka on the eve of our daring rescue attempt, I looked at the butterflies in amazement. *How could I live in a world with so much magic,* I thought, *and not know about it until a few months ago?* Amazing.

"Yeah, Tanaka," I said after he took the cage out of the closet. "How could I forget my own army?"

"Good boy, good boy!" he said. "Now, should we make them cockroaches, just for fun?"

"How about let's not and say we did. Are you guys tired? It's still morning where I just came from, so I don't feel like going to bed."

"Sleep?" he asked, his eyebrows lifted in surprise. "No time for sleep. We must figure out the rescue."

And we did. We spent the next few hours coming up with a plan.

And it was brilliant.

CHAPTER 12

Going on a Drive

The next morning, with a birdcage full of butterflies in tow, we set off for Mount Fuji. Nothing like having an army of winged shadow-beasts take over your planet to help you appreciate some of the things you used to take for granted—we didn't realize what a time we would have trying to get around.

The main source of transportation in Japan was the train system, which had finally, amidst all the chaos, ceased to operate completely. In fact, most of everything had shut down, with almost no services available. Every once in a while a taxi would drive by, but usually the driver looked way too terrified to pull over. Plus, most of the streets were jammed with cars whose owners had fallen asleep while driving.

Therefore, our immediate challenge was to get to the mountain in the first place. And for that, Tanaka had no qualms about stealing a car from one of its sleeping owners.

"Jeez, Tanaka," I said as he pulled a nice sleeping gentleman out of a shiny red car so small I thought we'd never fit the butterflies in the backseat. "You really have become a thief in your old age."

"Ah, Jimmy-san," he said with a grunt as he practically threw the man onto the sidewalk, "you no worry. Things like that matter nothing, now. You think Sleepyhead here complain when we save him from Stompers?"

"Good point," I said, and meant it.

We put the items needed for our plan in the trunk, helped Hood into the backseat with the *okisaru* and then took off toward the mountain, with Tanaka driving like a drunken senior citizen. He swerved around the many stopped cars, often having to go onto the sidewalk to get around them. Several times he honked, knowing full well that it would do no good. I wished over and over that I could take over the wheel, even though it would be my first time ever.

It wasn't long before we came to our next obstacle.

Gas. It got low just as we were reaching the outskirts of the main city.

We pulled into a gas station, but it was abandoned, just like the rest we had seen. Thanks to modern technology, we couldn't get it to work without the whole place up and running. Even if the automatic part for which you used a credit card had been working, none of us had one anyway. Tanaka mumbled something about how he would never trust a bank with his money.

"Yeah," I said, "I'm sure they were just knocking your door down every day to get to *all* your money too."

"What, that another funny Jimmy joke?" he asked. "Tanaka have more money than you dream about, stinky pants. Now, let me show you how smart I am."

He motioned for Hood to get out of the backseat, carrying the butterflies, and then Tanaka got our stuff out of the trunk. We followed him as he went to look into some of the cars around us in the streets. Soon, he yelled out.

"This one almost full!"

"Wow," I said as we got into the new car, a silver one that was a little bigger. "You really are smart to figure out we should switch cars when the other one runs out of gas." I smiled to let him know I didn't really mean to be such a smart aleck—I was just mad that I didn't think of it first.

"Oh, yes," he replied. "Uncle Tanaka very smart. Very smart man."

And so it was that we sped out of the city, heading toward the distant, snowcapped mountain that I had seen in a million pictures. Its upside-down conical shape was so familiar, and yet it was hard to believe I was actually looking at it in real life. It was much more impressive up close and personal. The further we got from the city, the fewer cars there were to swerve around, and so my stomach settled a bit, and I got very drowsy.

A thought hit me. "Why didn't we just use the Bender Ring to get there?"

Tanaka looked back at Hood, and then he answered for him. "We still not sure exactly where to go, so the Ring not much help."

"It could've at least gotten us close to it," I said.

"But maybe no cars up there, *neh*?"

"Yeah, I guess you're right. Mind if I sleep a little?"

"You go right ahead. Watch out for Stompers!"

It was meant to be a joke, but it made me ill. The last thing I remembered before sleep was Tanaka laughing in his usual nerve-grinding way, but I was so tired I didn't care.

When I woke up, Tanaka and Hood were standing outside in front of the car, looking at something in the distance. We were parked on the side of a narrow road, a towering wall of green to our left, an incredible view of the city to our right. The sun was high in the afternoon sky, but you could barely see it through the gray stain of the Ka.

I rubbed my eyes, and wondered how long I'd been asleep. It felt like forever, but it seemed I was more tired than when I started. Groggy and a little dizzy, I opened the door and got out.

"What're you guys looking at?"

"Jimmy-san," Tanaka said, "do you remember your Papa Fincher talk about how he can sense the Shadow Ka? The black haze?"

"Yeah."

"Well, very dark haze over there."

He pointed up ahead, where the road curved back toward the city to go around a massive cliff that jutted out from the main mountain. In the middle of the cliff side facing us, a long waterfall fell from a large crevice near the top. It widened as it fell until it was thirty or forty feet at the bottom, where it smashed into some rocks before flowing under a bridge and down toward the city.

Above the waterfall, the cloudy haze of the Shadow Ka was thicker, like a brewing storm cloud, dark and gloomy. Tendrils of black mist hung from the cloud like moss, reaching for the bottom of the waterfall.

"So . . . you think that's where they are?" I asked.

Hood knelt down and painted a few words on the pavement.

"WE'VE BEEN DRIVING AROUND THE MOUNTAIN FOR TWO HOURS. THE GRAYNESS IS STRONGEST HERE."

A chill went up my back as the reality of what we had set out to do sunk in. Until that moment, it had almost been like a fun day trip with two very strange friends. I was almost enjoying the adventure of it. But seeing that darkness again, knowing what terrible things it represented, brought back the fear and the panic.

"So . . . what do we do?"

Tanaka laughed. "We drive over there and go hiking."

"I was afraid you would say that."

As we got back in the car, I thought to voice a question I'd been scared to ask for a long time.

"Hood," I said as I turned in my seat to face him, "A long time ago, when we were in the mountains looking for you after the Pointing Finger, Rayna told me there was something . . . special about you. She made it clear that I shouldn't look at you without your robe."

Hood shifted in his seat, as if the conversation had given him a bad case of hemorrhoids. Tanaka put the car into drive and pulled back onto the road, heading for the waterfall up ahead.

"Well," I continued, "granted, I wasn't particularly excited to see you naked, but I got the feeling that wasn't the reason Rayna made me stay back. Plus, I'm sure you have other clothes on under that thing." I paused. "Uh . . . right?"

Hood shifted again, facing the window to his right.

"Okay, forget the whole naked thing—just tell me, or Tanaka, you tell me. What's up with Hood? Who is he really and why does he wear the robe?"

Tanaka said nothing, and stared straight ahead.

"Tanaka, come on. It's gotta be something really weird to shut you up like that."

"Not my decision," he replied. "You talk to Hood, leave me out."

"Hood?" I turned to him again. I didn't want to be rude, but he had become such a close friend, I felt I deserved to know the truth. Hood's pale hand appeared out of the folds of his robe, and he gripped the Bender Ring at his side like a security blanket. Then he reached forward and patted Tanaka on the shoulder.

Understanding Hood's signal that it was okay to tell me the secret, Tanaka sighed. He slowed the car down a bit and then spoke two words with a soft whisper.

"He dead."

Tanaka looked back to the road ahead of him, and said nothing more. His words skidded through my brain for a few seconds but made no sense.

"Dead?" I asked. "What do you mean?" I let out a courtesy laugh, trying to force Tanaka to tell me he was just kidding. His face didn't crack a bit, and he turned to me, his expression solemn and cold.

"Jimmy-san. The Hooded One is a ghost."

CHAPTER 13

Robed Death

"A *ghost?* What is that supposed to mean?"

"We don't know much. All Hood told us is that he thought he died, killed by terrible men, and then woke up in the same place but as ghost. He find robe, rest is history."

"A ghost?" I repeated. "But his hands . . . I've felt his body through the robe. How can he be a ghost?"

"Hard to explain. This is the form he takes. Not like ghost from spooky stories."

"As usual, Tanaka, you've cleared it right up."

A feeling of sickness invaded my stomach, and bile slimed the back of my throat. There was no doubt in my mind about Tanaka's words, and I knew he wasn't joking. It had to be true, as creepy as it made me feel. I turned my head slowly around to look at the dead man in the backseat. He sat there, his head hanging low, and a rush of shame filled my heart.

I knew that I loved him, just like I loved my mom and dad. And yet I was treating him like some kind of outcast, some kind of freak. The world had changed for me, and one more thing that was crazy shouldn't have made me feel such a way about a friend.

"Hood, I'm . . . sorry. I didn't . . ." No words would come to me, my mind numb with shock.

Hood lifted his head, and then reached forward to grab my hand. The touch of his skin was ice cold, and seemed to have a hint of electricity in it, or something that made my arm tingle. It was the touch of a dead person. A dead person who was somehow alive. I decided it was too much to try and figure out.

"Hood, you . . . and this goofy Japanese guy are two of my best friends in the whole world. Sorry if I made you feel bad." I shrugged. "Makes no difference to me if you're a dead guy."

It was surely one of the dumbest things I'd ever said in my life, but I think he understood.

Five seconds later, something landed on top of our car, and all thoughts of walking dead men left my head.

CHAPTER 14

Flying Car

The center of the roof, right behind my head, dented in several inches with a loud clank of crushing metal. Tanaka yelled out and almost lost control of the car, swerving to the edge of the other side of the road. Another thump above us was followed by a louder smash into the metal roof, caving it in near the Hooded One, even further than the first one. Hood sank lower in his seat, clasping the Bender Ring to him.

Another hit from above, and then another one. The roof of the car was being pummeled by something big and terrible. Tanaka yelled for us to hang on and kept driving, veering the car left and right, trying to shake off whatever was attacking us.

A loud crash next to my head made me jump, the window shattering into a million pieces. The fragments bounced off me as the Shield kicked in its power. Another boom sounded to my left, Tanaka's window splintering with a loud crack. Immediately, both of the windows in the backseat were smashed to pieces. Then the back window. Hood cowered, his pale, deathly hands covering his head.

61

"Hood!" I yelled. "Use the Ring! Get out of here!"

Before I could say anything more, something black appeared from above in the now windowless back of the car. It was the fully formed head of a Shadow Ka, looking at me with its eyes of darkness. Its mouth opened and let out a piercing scream, exploding the last window left in the car, the front windshield. Then its hands appeared, and it started crawling from above into the car, reaching for Hood.

With a quick thought, I called upon the Ice. A swirling string of mist solidified at once into the hard stuff and blasted the Ka away. I could see it tumbling over and over as the car left it behind. Amazingly, Tanaka was still driving, still swerving, snapping his head back and forth to see what was happening.

Another Ka appeared in the back, screaming its fury. Then one poked its head down on the side. Then one on the other side. I shot balls of Ice at them, but they ducked away. Their shadowed, clawed hands appeared, gripping the edges of the top of the car. I knew what they were going to try, because I'd seen them do it before.

"Tanaka! Slam on the brakes!"

But it was too late. Just as he pushed his foot hard against the pedal, the car lifted from the ground. The Ka tilted it heavily to my side, and Tanaka slammed into me, the Shield throwing him backward. Then they tilted us the other way, but I stayed put because I had my seat belt on. I could hear Hood and the birdcage bouncing back and forth behind me. The Ka shook the car, bounced it, tilted it over and over in all directions.

It hit me what they were doing, and it was working. They were trying to keep me confused—trying to prevent me from settling down and using my Gifts to stop them. Steeling myself, I put my mind to figuring out what I should do.

I reached down and unfastened my seat belt. The Ka were shooting for the sky, carrying us higher and higher. I yelled at Hood and Tanaka to hold on, and then I reached for the dashboard in front of me. I shifted my weight onto my feet and pushed myself forward and up through the front window. I grabbed the outer edge of the top of the car; then I turned myself around and sat down on the hood, my head now above the roof and facing the three Shadow Ka flying us away. I tightened my hold to steady myself.

The Ka screamed, shattering the air with their horrible sound. But I knew that they knew it was over. Their only hope was that I couldn't save my friends.

With a flurry of thought, I sent all three of them to oblivion in an explosion of ice and wind. The car stopped, seeming to freeze in midair with them gone. Then it yawned toward the front engine, where it was heaviest, and started falling back to earth.

My stomach tried to jump up my throat, and the sudden speed of our descent took me by surprise. My fingers slipped from the edge of the window and my whole body slid out of the car.

Free-falling, I stared in horror as the car carrying my friends slipped out of reach.

We were only seconds from smashing into the mountainside. Butterflies flew out of the windows in droves. I shot a stream of Ice toward the top of the car, connecting my arm to it, and then shrank it as fast as my mind would let me. The cold rope pulled my whole body and slammed me into the car, the Shield making it rebound slightly. I froze my hand to the metal of the roof and kicked my feet through the front window, felt my left foot touch the passenger seat.

The ground rushed up at us, the whole of it filling my peripheral vision.

Tanaka grabbed my leg, squeezing tight, knowing the Shield would expand and protect him. I had to get to Hood. "Grab on!" I yelled to him.

Grasping the steering wheel, I tried to pull the rest of my body into the car. But now I was upside down, the ground only feet away. I could see the jagged rocks waiting to tear us apart. With a last grunt of effort, I threw all of my strength into lifting myself into the car.

But it was too late. The car smashed into the side of the mountain. Metal crumpled all around us as the Shield protected Tanaka and me. My mind screamed out in hope— hope that Hood would grab me in that last split second.

A spark ignited the spewing gasoline, and the world around us exploded in a blast of heat and light. Tanaka held on as the Shield expanded into a perfect sphere of protection, keeping us safe from the fire and twisted metal.

But there was no sign of Hood.

CHAPTER 15

Ghost or No Ghost

The sickening smell of burning gas, the sounds of warping metal, the occasional explosion of something new—it filled the air around us. Hugging, Tanaka and I walked away from the destruction, the Shield moving flame and metal out of our way as we walked. Soon we were clear of it, and the fresh air that hit us was like coming out of the pool after a contest to see who could stay underwater the longest.

In the air above, hundreds of *okisaru* flew in a tight swarm, waiting for a command from Tanaka. I hoped they all had escaped.

We kept walking until we were far enough away to be safe. We collapsed to the ground near a patch of trees on the slope, exhausted. My heart ached with the thought of losing Hood, especially knowing that I could have saved him. If I had just waited to get rid of the Shadow Ka . . .

I got up and walked back to the wreckage, even though I knew there was no way he could have survived, ghost or no ghost. Unless he pulled a Casper and flew away at the last second. *How does that work, anyway?* I thought. *How does a ghost die if it's already dead?*

I walked around and through the burning mess, the Shield protecting me like usual. I kicked pieces of the car and let the Shield move some of the heavier ones aside so I could get a good look. I couldn't find signs of him anywhere.

Nothing. Wait a minute . . .

Nothing. The light went on in my head. There was no sign of Hood, no sign of his robe, no sign of the . . .

I sensed someone behind me, and a smile lit up my face. Of course. I turned around, knowing full well who it was before I saw him. He had taken my advice after all, and used the Bender Ring to get the heck out of that flying car.

I gave Hood the biggest hug I could, ignoring the fact that it wasn't even a real body I had my arms around.

After scouting around for more Shadow Ka, we sat down on an outcropping of rock looking over the valley. Exhausted both mentally and physically, we needed a break. And we needed to talk about what to do next.

"Our plan is dead," said Tanaka. "Dead like Hood here!"

"Why?" I asked.

Tanaka threw his hands up in frustration. "What you mean, why? You think those black buzzards not go and tell their friends we here? Our whole plan, dead."

"You think they survived? I'm sure they're lying dead down there somewhere."

"So what? Even if they dead, they have others nearby who saw everything. I promise you that."

He had a good point. Before I could think of a reply, Hood got up on his knees and started painting on the rock.

"THIS MAY HELP US."

I raised my eyebrows, knowing that he would explain what he meant.

"THINK. NOW IT WILL WORK EVEN BETTER." Hood had to shuffle a few feet over to keep writing. "NOW THEY KNOW WE ARE IN THE AREA. NOW IT SEEMS MORE NATURAL WHEN WE PLAY OUR TRICK."

"He's right, Tanaka," I said. "Before, they might've been suspicious that we just happened to show up—they might've seen through our plan. I think Hood's right."

"Unless," said Tanaka, "they know each Shadow Ka, each one, individually."

Another good point. Raspy had once told me that the Ka shared their minds somehow—that they could communicate and exchange thoughts and feelings in a way that we would never understand. But the more I thought about our plan, the more perfect it seemed.

"If the *okisaru* can truly do what you say they can, it will work."

"Why you say that?"

"Just trust me." I stood up and stretched my arms and legs, letting out a yawn worthy of lion-roar status. "Come on. The road is just up that ridge, and we couldn't have strayed too far from where we saw the waterfall. The black haze is thick up there."

I offered a hand to both of them, and soon we were on our way.

As we clambered up the side of the densely forested mountain, it grew darker as the taint above grew thicker. When we reached the road, I looked up into the gloomy sky. The black cloud-like haze seethed and boiled like a fast-motion storm, and it reminded me of a story Joseph once told me.

When he first went into the Blackness, the Givers showed him a world that had been completely taken over by the Stompers. All he'd seen was a sea of stone beds with covered, humped shapes sleeping in the Coma. The entire world had been covered in a blanket of dark, gray clouds. Now we knew why, and could see the same darkness taking over our own world.

Without a word, we crossed the narrow road and entered the brush on the other side, heading for the waterfall. The roar of the falls was getting louder, and the air seemed to grow more damp as we approached it through the thick vegetation. Tanaka's arms were scratched and bruised from the endless branches and pointy twigs, and Hood's robe kept getting snagged left and right. The Shield made it easy for me, opening up a path as I moved forward.

How did I ever live without this thing? I asked myself.

After a half-hour or so of hiking, we broke through into a clearing, and the mighty falling wall of water appeared in front of us. The boom and crash of the falls hitting the jagged rocks along the bottom was loud as a freight train. A fine spray of mist filled the air around us, instantly matting my hair to my head and soaking my clothes. A quick look around revealed no Shadow Ka, at least not in plain sight.

Worried we had come too far, I hurried back into the cover of the woods, motioning Tanaka and Hood to follow.

"You guys ready?" I asked. "Hood, do you know where to go?"

He nodded, and then I turned to Tanaka. Only four butterflies had come along, the rest ordered to wait in a place of safety back near the road. They rested on Tanaka's shoulders, their wings moving back and forth ever so slowly.

"Are you ready, General Tanaka?"

I expected some type of joke, but he nodded his head without a word or smile. Then he barked out something in Japanese, and the butterflies took flight. I couldn't wait to see what would happen next.

With the same flash of light, the same trailing blur of brightness, the *okisaru* began their transformation. Our entire plan depended on it.

Right before our eyes, they turned themselves into Shadow Ka.

CHAPTER 16

The Plan Begins

It was hard to repress the feeling of terror that filled my heart at seeing four Ka standing in the woods next to us. They were seven feet tall, blacker than the depths of space, huge wings folded back behind their bodies. Their faces reminded me of dragons, although their features were obscured in the strange shadowy substance of which they were made. Long, thick arms ended in black claws, as did their short but stocky legs.

They were horrible, and therefore perfect.

"Tanaka, have them scream," I said. "Make sure they can talk to the other Ka."

He said a few words to the transformed *okisaru,* and they all screamed as one, shattering the air like invisible lightning. The suddenness and sheer power of it made me fall back onto the ground. Tanaka said something else, and all four of them flapped their massive wings, lifting themselves up into the trees. Then they came back down, and looked at me. A racing shiver of fear swept across my body, but I forced it away. As terrible as these guys looked, they were on my side.

I got up and brushed myself off.

"Let's go then, before these fellas make me wet my pants."

Two of the Ka-disguised *okisaru* went over and grabbed Hood, one arm each, like secret service agents helping the president's grandma through a metal detector. The other two did the same to Tanaka. I could tell already that they were being way too gentle.

"Tanaka," I said, "they need to play the part."

"You always right, Jimmy-san." He yelled out another order.

The *okisaru* hesitated, and Tanaka said it again. One of them let out a sharp screech, and then they obeyed. They grabbed Tanaka and Hood more roughly, and began to stomp through the woods toward the waterfall, dragging their fake captives along like cops after a drug raid. I followed, hoping against hope that our plan went off without a hitch.

It would all depend on the little secret I had learned in the Storm World.

The falls were way bigger than they'd looked from the road. As we approached, I felt like some giant had scooped up the entire ocean into a bucket and decided he wanted to dump it on our heads. The *okisaru* dragged and pushed Hood and Tanaka around its outermost edge, and then headed to the dark space between the mountain and the wall of falling water. All of us slipped a time or two on the wet rocks, and by the time we reached the cold stone of the mountainside, we were soaked to the bone.

Years of erosion had created a huge abscess in the side of

the cliff, so that there was a large pool behind the curtain of the waterfall. It was odd to see it from the back side. The water was smoother, almost like a sheet of glass. For some reason the froth and the mist and the spray were not nearly as prevalent on the inside. It was one of the coolest things I'd ever seen.

We waded into the black pool and headed to the back of the cave. The water came to our knees, and the bottom was littered with rocks set at all sorts of uncomfortable angles, making it difficult to walk. We stumbled and bumbled our way across, and then reached a narrow tunnel that shot into the face of the towering mountain.

Two Shadow Ka stood at the entrance, guarding their hideout. They came forward, yelping out a few screams that of course made no sense to me. Our *okisaru* answered back, and pushed Tanaka and Hood into the water in front of them. Then they all screamed, the echo of it piercing my ears. I just stood there, anxious with worry, waiting to see if my part of the plan worked.

One of the guards stepped forward, scanning with its hidden eyes the entire area, looking to see if anyone else had followed. It eyes passed over me several times, but it made no movement of recognition or surprise. Then, satisfied and excited to show its master this new development—these new prisoners, the Ka turned and headed for the tunnel, motioning the others to follow.

It had worked. The Shield was making me invisible.

With a sigh of relief, I followed them into the darkness of the mountain.

So far, so good.

CHAPTER 17

Into the Mountain

The tunnel stretched on forever, or at least it seemed like it. The walls of the long passage were black rock, jagged and rough, like it had been dug out by men with no care for things that looked nice. The floor was smooth, as if it had been traveled for years by a secret people who had never seen the sun. Every forty feet or so a light bulb hung from the ceiling by a rope, with no sign of wiring or other source of power. They let off a faint glow, and swayed back and forth in a warm breeze that came from somewhere ahead, creating angled, dancing shadows on the walls.

The whole place smelled like wet dog, rot, and decay. I kept a slight distance behind the others, and the stench worsened the farther we went. Although I had no reason to know for sure, the smell made me think of decomposing bodies. All in all, it was a real pleasant place to be—if you were a vampire or zombie.

The tunnel made a turn to the right, and then began to make a slow descent. From that point it seemed to go downward in a steady, wide spiral. We had walked for at least an hour, maybe two, and my legs were aching. The look of the tunnel and the horrible smell never changed, and the magic light bulbs never ceased shining.

Down we went. Down, down, into the depths of whatever world waited below the mountain.

Up ahead, one of the Ka screamed, and everyone came to a stop. I moved forward, more confident in my invisibility, anxious to see what was happening. The wonder of the First Gift, the fact that it could not only protect me from bullets and fists but actually repel others' sight still amazed me. And made me very, very thankful.

The group had reached a place where the tunnel ended in a massive stone wall with a hole in the middle, and one of the Ka was looking through the hole. It screamed again, and then the rumbling sound of heavy stone grinding against stone filled the air. The wall was not a wall—it was a door, and it was swinging open.

Tanaka looked back and caught my eyes. I quickly shook my head, scared that he would give something away. His face betrayed how scared and nervous he felt. With a look of dejection, he turned back toward the stone door.

With a loud boom, the door slammed into the wall of the tunnel. A reddish light came from the opening, and the Shadow Ka moved the small company out of the tunnel and into whatever lay beyond. They weren't even all the way through before the massive door began to close. I hurried and ran forward as it swung closed. It came to a rest with a loud boom.

We stood on a wide ledge that jutted out from the door into open air. From both sides of the ledge, a set of stairs curved down and out of sight. My curiosity overcame my fear, and I stepped to the side of where everyone else stood, and walked up to the edge of the landing.

My eyes tried to tell me what I was seeing, but I couldn't believe it.

We were at the very top of a cavern so large that it seemed to break every known rule of physics or natural law. It stretched forward and beyond even what I could see, as if we had reached the center of the earth and it had been hollowed out like the pit from a peach. For miles and miles there was open air, and the bottom of the cavern lay far below, the stairs to our sides winding down to the bottom with what must've been thousands of steps. Along the sides of the cavern I could see other openings similar to the one from which we'd just come, all with the same set of twin staircases leading to the bottom.

All of them were full of Shadow Ka. And all of the Ka were carrying human bodies, whether dead or asleep, I couldn't tell for sure. But my gut told me they were alive and in the Coma of the Stompers. I leaned over and tried to see the bottom, to see where they were carrying all of those people.

It was far, far below me, but I still knew in an instant what was down there, covering the width and breadth of the entire cavern floor.

Thousands upon thousands of rectangular blocks of stone. Stone beds. And most of them were occupied.

CHAPTER 18

Large Bedroom

I jumped when the Ka next to me let out a piercing wail. The group then headed for the staircase to the left and began the long descent to the bottom. Tanaka and Hood were exhausted, dragged along more than led now. I felt so bad for them, and frustrated, knowing that I had the ability to rescue them with almost no effort.

But I knew that was not an option. We had come for our other friends, for Rayna and Miyoko. But what if they were deep in the Coma—what if we were too late? My heart sinking lower by the minute, I stepped back from the edge and followed the sordid company down the stairs.

The stone beneath our feet was dusty and covered with loose rocks. The cut stairs were wide but not very deep, making the trip down a cumbersome one because of the constant need to watch my step. As I followed the Ka, some real and some impostors, down toward the bottom of the cavern, my thoughts turned to the next phase of our plan. The hard part would be finding our friends amidst the countless victims below.

The trip down took even longer than I'd thought it would.

Switchback after switchback, hundreds after hundreds of stairs, down we went. The ceiling of the cavern hung above us like storm clouds made of earth, defying all sense of what should be physically possible. It made my head spin when I looked up, and so I refocused my sights on what awaited us below.

As we got closer, the sheer numbers of Shadow Ka and people became more apparent, and more staggering. I tried to think of a time when I had seen so many people in one place. The first thing that came to mind was when I had been very little, and the Braves had won the World Series. A few days after that there had been a parade in Atlanta, and my family watched from the top of a ten-story building. For as far as I could see, thousands of people had been packed in the streets—a sea of bodies in every direction. I knew without a doubt that there were more people in the cavern than I had seen that day.

Except for one big difference. Most of the ones I saw now were in a deep sleep.

More than half of the stone beds were occupied, the people lying flat on their backs, eyes closed. No tubes or IVs or anything were attached to them, and I wondered how the Ka kept them all alive.

The Ka were carrying countless others to the empty beds, their lifeless bodies slumped over the black shoulders of their captors, flopping with each heavy step. Many Ka also carried bodies in their huge talons, flying to and fro. It all looked like some massive production plant, with the workers participating in organized chaos. It made me sick.

My resolve deepened, and I swore to myself that we would win this war.

We were coming upon the last few stairs when one of the Ka from the floor below noticed our group and walked toward us. He was bigger than the others, and the way other Ka deferred to his movements gave him a sense of authority. Our group came to a stop, and waited for the big Ka to speak. The constant sounds of screaming Ka, flapping wings, and shuffling feet had made the whole place loud and irritating up until now, but everything seemed to quiet down in that moment.

The leader Ka looked over Tanaka and Hood, his interest in these new prisoners very high. His black eyes passed over me as well, and I couldn't help but hold my breath in fear that maybe he could see what the others could not. But if he did, he made no sign of it. Then something strange happened. The air around his black skin wavered, like heat waves coming off a flame.

Then he began to change.

His body seemed to draw back in on itself, shrinking into a smaller version of a Shadow Ka. The blackness of his skin ebbed into lines all over his body, leaving gray skin behind. His wings shrunk until they disappeared, and his features melted and morphed into those of a human. The black lines receded until they were gone.

Seconds later, what had been a Ka was now a human being again. And I knew this man, although he looked even more evil than the last time I'd seen him, when I'd blasted him away from our ship on the ocean with a burst of Ice.

It was Kenji, leader of the Bosu Zoku.

CHAPTER 19

Japanese Spit

Tanaka must have been as shocked as I was based on Kenji's first words.

"Yes, Tanaka-san," he said. "We have the fortune of meeting once again." He took a step forward and lightly touched Tanaka's face. "For your sake, I want to appear in my lesser form, so we can talk and share stories. Do you like my trick? Does it make you feel more comfortable?"

Tanaka spit in Kenji's face. I almost wanted to yell out and cheer him on.

Kenji laughed as he wiped the gray spittle from his cheek. "Yes. Now I know why it is that your breath reeks of death, my fellow countryman. It's in your very saliva." He barked out another laugh, and it reminded me of some cheap movie where the bad guy always lets out his evil chortle.

"You have caught us, yes," said Tanaka. "But what good are we? You don't have the boy, and Jimmy-san all that matters."

Kenji's eyes focused in on Tanaka's, like he was trying to read some deeper meaning from the words. Then his smile returned.

"My friend, I know of his weaknesses. We can always count on your hero to put the lives of his meaningless friends before the fate of the world. We have you, we have others. We have killed most of the Alliance. The more I can make Jimmy waste his time on finding insignificant bugs like you, the greater our chances of success. Don't you see? His time has almost run out. Our victory is all but assured."

"You count eggs before they chickens," said Tanaka, and I winced at his bad attempt to use an American phrase.

"I think you mean chickens before they hatch, you idiot," said Kenji. "You should've paid more attention in school."

"Whatever. It not over. This I promise."

Kenji quit smiling and replaced it with a mocking frown. "Your word means a lot to me, Tanaka. Come. I will let you cry your promises to my masters as you feed them with your fear." He snapped his fingers, and motioned toward the endless sea of beds behind him. "I've saved your daughter and your friend for when you arrived." The smile came back.

"It's time for all of you to sleep."

The *okisaru* holding Hood and Tanaka followed Kenji as he turned and walked away from the stairs. After a few seconds, his body vibrated and then quickly morphed back into the full and hideous shape of a Shadow Ka. His great wings flailed behind him and whipped in the air to show his power. He led the group through a hundred or so occupied stone beds. I looked down at the sorry people as we walked, searching for signs of life.

Their chests rose and fell ever so slightly, and their skin

seemed pale and damp. Their eyes shifted back and forth under closed lids, and every once in a while their heads would jerk to the left or right. But that was not what was most disturbing.

All of their faces looked terrified, a permanent scowl of fear and anguish dominating their features. I couldn't imagine what was going on inside their minds.

Kenji stopped in front of two empty beds, and motioned to them with his claws. Then he screamed a command to the *okisaru* holding Tanaka and Hood.

Improvising well, the fake Shadow Ka dragged the two humans forward and threw them onto the stone blocks. Knowing there was no point in resisting, they didn't attempt to escape or get up from the beds.

"Dad!" someone yelled from several beds away.

Miyoko.

She was there, she was alive. A Ka held her captive, dragging her along, and Rayna was with her, also alive and well. The Ka had wanted everyone to be there, to share in the misery of the Stompers at the same time. It was sick and cruel, but we knew that's what they'd do. And our plan depended on it.

The Shadow Ka pulled and yanked on Miyoko and Rayna and brought them over to two stone blocks next to Tanaka and Hood. Without a care, they threw them onto the beds.

"Jimmy!" yelled Rayna to Tanaka. "Is Jimmy okay?" She still hadn't noticed me, standing as I was behind all the others.

The Ka nearest her slapped Rayna on the head, and she fell onto her back. She lay silent.

"Yes," Tanaka replied.

A scream from Kenji shut everyone up for good. He began to roar a constant screeching of sounds, and I knew in an instant what he was doing.

It was the song of the Shadow Ka. The spell that made people fall into the Coma, the preparation for the Stompers to enter their minds. We all knew what to do.

Tanaka's eyes rolled into the back of his head, and then his eyelids began to close. Hood swayed to the right and put his pale hands over the place his eyes would be. Rayna closed hers. I closed mine. Four *okisaru* that looked just like Shadow Ka brought great wings up to shield their eyes.

It was time.

A light brighter than the sun exploded out of nowhere, and our plan went into action.

CHAPTER 20

Eye Shine

Tanaka had never really told me all of the details about how and when Miyoko and Rayna were kidnapped by the Shadow Ka. Hood and Tanaka had gone looking for them, and had found them just as a massive raid by the Ka intercepted their efforts. Without being able to get to me, our enemy's second alternative was to get the next best thing—those who were close to me, in hopes of using them as collateral.

What happened during that raid was terrible—so bad that Tanaka found it hard to talk about. But I did know that most of the Alliance—whom Rayna and Miyoko had worked so hard to gather and reunite—had been killed. The only reason those two survived is because they were useless against me if they were dead. If anything, it would only increase my efforts to get payback.

In those tense moments, when Tanaka and Hood barely escaped while they watched the almost unbearable act of seeing their loved ones taken, Tanaka had been able to get a note to Miyoko by using one of the *okisaru*. It had said, "We will come for you. When you are ready, use your eyes."

And that was what she had just done.

All of the members of the Alliance had a gift. Some had more than others. Miyoko's was the ability to shine unfathomable light from her eyes, a power that defied any common sense I had in my little brain. The source of that light was a complete mystery—another one of the millions I'd chalked up in the last few months of my life. But it had come in handy before, and it worked perfectly as a beacon for all of us to begin our actions at the same time.

No one but us expected it. Just as she felt the first tingle of sleep flow through her, Miyoko opened her eyes and exerted the full force of her Gift, throwing all of her power into it like she'd never done before. Compared to the relative darkness of the cavern, the light that burst forth from her eyes was like the brilliance of the sun after an eclipse.

As the place seemed to erupt into flames, Kenji's song was halted in an instant. With a different scream than before, one of agony, he pulled his wings over his beastly head and fell to the ground. All around us the other Shadow Ka did the same, falling left and right, dropping human bodies from their grasp, screeching and wailing.

We waited for a few more seconds, knowing that Miyoko would end it soon.

The light disappeared. Even though our eyes had been closed or covered, it was still like walking into a theater from outside on a bright, sunny day. It was hard to make out much at all, but every second was precious, and we sprung into action.

Everything happened at once.

CHAPTER 21

Beds Arise

While Kenji and the other Shadow Ka wallowed in their temporary blindness, the four *okisaru* jumped forward and grabbed Miyoko, Rayna, Tanaka, and Hood—one apiece. They grasped them in their huge shadow claws and immediately took flight into the vast space of the open cavern. Even as they did so, Kenji stood and shook off the short-lived daze caused by Miyoko's light. The other Ka around him were also recovering, and it didn't take long before they realized what was going on.

Meanwhile, I called upon the Ice and formed a huge tower of it under my feet, raising me into the air forty or fifty feet. Then, with a thought, I pulled in the power of the Shield and released myself from invisibility. I wanted them all to see me now, and I wanted them to assume much more than what had actually happened. It was time they really and truly feared me beyond even what they should.

Their body language revealed the surprise of seeing me appear out of nowhere, standing above them on a tower of Ice. A deathly silence came over the place, and they all stared.

With a voice as loud as I could boom out of my innards, I began to speak.

"It's over, Kenji! It's over, all of you! Your mindless devotion to the Stompers is useless and it's time to end!" I shot a slew of Ice at Kenji to make my point. Just before it reached him, I made it melt and devour him and then freeze again, encompassing him in a huge ball of frozen water. His body stood rigid in a position of defense, his mouth open, clawed hands reaching forward, his wings stretching out to take flight. The other Ka stared and stayed silent.

And then came the real kicker. I knew it was a long shot, but I had to try it, to spread the word before everything came to a head in the days to come.

"All of you are still human, deep down inside! You can see that I'm gaining in power every day! You have one more chance to come back before the end! Take it, because the day is coming when everything will be decided once and for all!"

With a buildup of more Ice below, I made the tower grow another twenty feet higher.

"In the end, only one side will be the right one!"

I closed my eyes, knowing that what I did next would be the hardest thing I'd done so far. Straining my mind, throwing every ounce of thought and will and energy into the power of my Gift, I pictured the thousands of stone blocks below, imagined Ice forming under and around them, building and building until the beds and those who rested on them were completely enclosed, isolated from the Ka.

Swishing and swirling sounds filled the cavern, and I knew the Ice had jumped into action. I looked down, and saw that everything had happened just as I'd envisioned it. Every stone bed in sight was encased in huge blocks of the cold stuff.

Every other time I'd used the Ice, it had always defied gravity—my control over it overpowering that nifty little law of nature. Counting on that, I lifted the thousands of blocks of Ice into the air. With a crackling thunder of creaks and groans, they broke contact with the hard stone floor and floated upward until they hovered, bobbing slightly, twenty feet from the ground. My heart pounded with the mental strain, my breath running ragged. The effort exerted on my brain fed to my muscles, and they grew taut, as if I were actually holding the beds up with my own strength. I knew I couldn't do this much longer, and panic filled me as I realized that maybe I'd bitten off more than I could chew.

But I didn't give up. Using my hands as symbolic guides, I directed the countless beds up and toward the cave that led to the outside. I'd never planned on taking things this far, but I knew I couldn't leave these people behind, left to endless hours of fear and torment inside their heads.

The ice-covered blocks shot upward, like an army of futuristic warships heading out to battle in the depths of space. My mind directed them as I looked, made them fall into order, forming into a single-file line as they flew toward the exit from the cavern.

But it had gone too far. My strength was gone.

Before even one block had entered the cave far above, I collapsed to my knees, the pressure and the strain too great.

The formation of stone beds stopped their flight, faltered in midair.

And then they began to fall.

CHAPTER 22

Icy Prayer

Time seemed to slow to a standstill. I fell onto my back, staring upward so that I could see the tragedy that I'd caused. Every one of the ice-covered beds had made it hundreds of feet into the air, and they were now plummeting to the cavern floor. It didn't take a genius to realize that when they crashed to the ground, those innocent lives they bore would be crushed and sent to their deaths.

Down they came, like a dumped load of bricks. Just to make it perfect, some of them were going to land on me. Of course the Shield would then protect me, and the irony of it all would be complete.

I closed my eyes, and without any strength left in my body, I made one last ditch effort to call upon the Ice. Almost treating it like a prayer, I asked it to take these people to safety outside.

My brain shut down from exhaustion, and all thoughts went black.

When I woke up, the tower of ice was gone. At least, I was no longer lying on it. Instead, I could feel the cold hard stone of the cavern floor below me. My head pounded and dizzying lights swam before my eyes as I rolled over onto my side and tried to pull myself together. I coughed and then rolled onto my back and rubbed my eyes and forehead. Everything was very dark, and I slowly made myself stand up, steadying myself against the sudden rush of nausea.

Seconds later, my eyes adjusted, and I saw what was around me.

Encircling me, only four or five feet away on all sides, was a pack of Shadow Ka. Behind them were more, and behind them even more. They went in all directions for as far as I could see, standing there, wings folded in, looking at me without exception. And they were all silent except the occasional snort or grunt, or the shuffling of wings and feet.

I did a slow three-sixty, turning and looking at all of them, wondering what was going on. What had happened to all those people on the beds? How long had I been out? A deep misery filled my chest, and my eyes watered with the coming of tears. Not only had I failed to scare them with my power, I'd made it worse. They would never come back to their human sides now that they had seen my limits. They would win.

"What!" I yelled, my voice choking up. "What do you want?"

I knew the Shield would protect me, and I felt no fear at all. But I didn't care anymore. Hope had seemed to abandon me without so much as an apology before it left. I fell back down to the ground and buried my head in my arms, wishing the Ka would just go away and leave me alone. But then something happened.

A strange noise arose—an indescribable one; one that made me think of wet clay being squished through fingers.

I poked my head up, and saw the source of the noise.

The Shadow Ka were morphing into humans.

In the semi darkness, their metamorphosis was nothing but a blur of movement and shadow, but soon there were no more Shadow Ka, only humans. They looked sick and pale, their clothes tattered and worn.

Their clothes. It hit me how bizarre it was that when they changed back into humans they had clothes on. It was the first time I'd thought of it. The Shadow Ka as beasts did not have clothes. So how did they when their bodies changed back?

One of them spoke, scattering my thoughts.

"Why do you stare at us like that?" he asked. It was a Japanese man, his black hair matted to his head and sweat covering the rest of him like varnish. His clothes were damp and I could smell his body odor from three feet away. It seemed turning into a Shadow Ka made for one heck of a day at the office.

"Why?" he continued. "Does it shock you that we don't *want* to be monsters? Do you think we enjoy having our lives taken over by those things?"

My head was having a hard time computing what he meant. Had they just removed themselves from the Ka—kicked them out?

"Are you . . . are you free?" I asked.

"I don't know," he moaned, a look of pain on his face.

"Most of our brothers, or what used to be our brothers, fled right after you fell. They somehow got Kenji out too. But those you see here, we listened to your message. We fought, and we gained our lives back. For now at least."

"Really?" It showed how little faith I had in my earlier message that I was so shocked it had worked on some of them. "You could hear me—it really worked?"

"Only time will tell."

I looked around at the dejected men and women, and saw that there were probably fifty or sixty of them. That meant that hundreds of others had not heard, or at least not listened.

"Can you help me?" I asked. "You may know a lot that could help us beat them once and for all."

The man shook his head, and then let out a forced laugh. "Don't look to us to win your war, boy. What can we do against the likes of those demons?"

"You can tell us how their minds work, how they think. Don't you know anything about their plans, or where others are gathered? Do you remember anything?"

"I'm sorry, we can't help you. Just go, and leave us. We have families to find, friends to gather. Before the end comes."

My pity for them turned to disbelief. "You're going to give up? After what you just did to escape from them?"

"Escape!" the man yelled, spitting all over me. "You think we've escaped? Better to be one of them than to live in the spell of the Stompers for the rest of eternity. Better to serve them than to feed them! You have no idea!" He turned, walked away a few steps, and then stopped, lowering his head to his chest.

"You cannot win, Jimmy Fincher. You cannot win."

He walked away toward a far staircase, and without a

word, the rest of them followed, silent and sullen.

"What's your name?" I yelled to him. He ignored me. "What's your name!"

He paused again, fifty feet away, and then turned toward me.

"My name is Sato. But soon I will not even have that."

And then he was gone, lost in the crowd.

CHAPTER 23

Up the Stairs

I watched them until they were halfway up the long staircase, full of a hurt that was new to me. I didn't know those people any more than I knew the president of Timbuktu. But to see the despair in their eyes, to know that they had lost all hope—it filled me with much of the same, and it was almost too much to bear.

I turned away, and began figuring out what I needed to do next.

Nearby there was a huge puddle of water, a small pond almost, that had collected in a large indentation in the rocky floor of the cavern. Figuring it was the residue of the melted tower of Ice I'd created, I looked around and tried to get my bearings.

It only took about two seconds for me to realize something that almost made me fall down.

There were no stone beds to be seen, anywhere. They were all gone.

Wondering where the energy came from, I burst into a full run and headed for the stairwell we'd come down earlier.

By the time I reached the top of the stairs, it felt like tiny dragons had invaded my body, burning me with their flames from the inside out. My heart was pumping, and sweat covered me from head to toe. I walked to the edge of the landing for one last look down into the cavern as I caught my breath, hands on my knees.

It was so different now. No stone blocks, no people, no Shadow Ka. The place was so empty it seemed even bigger than the first time I saw it, which I would've thought impossible. I couldn't help but wonder how the whole mountain didn't just collapse with this big hole in the middle of it.

I straightened up, and felt like I was leaving a place I'd spent half my life. So much had happened in such a short time, it was like a part of me would always stay there after I'd been long gone.

With legs like rubber, I reached deep down for some special Jimmy energy, and headed for the dark cave. The massive stone door was wide open, which was incredibly lucky, because I hadn't thought of it once until that very moment. *Who opened it?* I wondered, as I walked through the opening. *Did the Ice push it open?*

The odd light bulbs still worked, making the whole place look like the lair of some serial killer. Of course, that's exactly what the Ka and the Stompers were, I thought, except that they were doing something even worse. What they did to people was a *living* death. My body shuddered at the thought.

The tunnel wound its way up and up, and my legs cursed me the whole way. It had seemed long before but not *that* long.

I stumbled and fell. The Shield broke my fall. I found

myself wishing it could protect me from fatigue, but that was probably asking a bit much. Then it hit me that maybe I could make a chair out of Ice and float it along the tunnel with me sitting on it. With my mental state just as exhausted as my physical body, I didn't think it would work. Maybe a trick to try later.

On and on I climbed my way up the slowly ascending tunnel. On what seemed like my millionth step since leaving the cavern, I saw a brighter light ahead. Energized by the thought of getting out of that place, I stumbled forward. Soon I heard the sound of crashing water, and my heart jumped for joy.

I came upon the exit, and saw the pool of water beyond it and the backside of the cascading waterfall. The sun was hitting it dead on from the other side, shooting sparkling rays of light onto the face of the small lake, its reflection both beautiful and blinding. Especially after having been in the relative darkness of the cave for so long. With the disappearance of the Ka, the taint must have lessened considerably for the sun to be so bright. I shielded my eyes and stepped out of the mountain and into the cool water.

I stepped gingerly across the rocky bottom, knowing that my legs were almost shot, and headed for the side of the waterfall we'd come from originally. The spray of the falls felt so wonderful, and I reached down and brought some cool water to my mouth with both hands. The long trip had made me a little thirsty.

I climbed up onto the rocks beside the waterfall and into the full daylight.

My breathing stopped when I saw what was waiting for me.

CHAPTER 24

Reunion

It was hard to take it all in at once.

The first thing I noticed were the stone beds everywhere I looked—in the clearing, scattered among the trees, filling the mountain road, packed tightly together. And they were all occupied, the people still in their comas. There had to be some kind of magic associated with those stupid blocks of rock— something that helped keep those people asleep and fed and undisturbed.

My heart soared when I saw them, however, because it meant that at least they were still alive. The Ice had come through in a way I'd never imagined, answering my last desperate prayer before I'd lost consciousness. Once again, the power of my Gifts staggered my mind.

I continued to take in the bizarre scene that surrounded me.

Four people were tied up and hanging from nearby trees. They hung upside down, their feet attached to the trees by a rough-looking rope. Although the rising sun was shining right in my eyes, I could tell who three of them were. The fourth one was a mystery.

I ran down the slope of the open clearing and headed for the trees where they were captive. As I got closer, I realized they were also blindfolded and gagged, and I could only hope they were still alive. Before I had even reached the trees, I used the Ice to freeze and break apart their ropes. Then I let them down slowly with another rope made of Ice. A couple of grunts from someone let me know they were indeed alive.

Tanaka. Miyoko. Rayna. Some stranger.

But Hood was gone.

I quickly helped them up and broke off their gags and blindfolds before they could even try. Rayna doubled over and puked, the sudden transition from being upside down to right side up too much for her. Tanaka ran over and hugged Miyoko tight, and I joined them. It was especially good to see Miyoko and Rayna alive and well, since they were the whole point of us going there in the first place. The stranger stood to the side, quiet and reserved.

"What happened?" I asked.

Tanaka pointed to Rayna. "You tell, please." Then he resumed hugging his daughter, making sure she was okay.

Rayna came up to me. It had been a while since I'd seen her black hair and her scarred face and her green leather outfit. She was an odd duck, but she meant the world to me.

"The four *okisaru* brought us here," she said, "and soon after that the Icy stone blocks came flying out of the mountain. How did you do that?"

"I have no idea. It was the Ice—that's all I know."

Rayna shook her head. "You are an amazing creature, Jimmy Fincher."

"Yeah, yeah, I know. So what else happened?"

"Hundreds of Shadow Ka came flying out of the cave, screaming and yelling like they were extremely upset, which I'm sure they were. They attacked us, and we were helpless. But the rest of the *okisaru* showed up, turned into some kind of freaky flying lions or something, and started beating the Ka back. They chased them away and we haven't seen them or the *okisaru* since."

"Then how in the heck did you end up in the tree? And where's Hood?"

"Hood escaped with his Bender Ring. As for the tree, you can thank him for that," she replied, pointing to the stranger.

He walked up to me. He was a young man, not much older than I, dressed in jeans and a sweatshirt. His hair was blond and scraggly, and his face was covered in the beginnings of a beard. He looked like any normal kid you'd see on his way to high school, late for class because he'd slept in.

"Who are you?" I asked, realizing too late that I'd been was kind of rude.

He held out his hand. I took it, and he gave me a firm handshake.

"My name is Justin." He turned to the others, gave a mocking smile, and then motioned to them.

"But they call me The Half."

CHAPTER 25

Bad Nickname

"The Half?" I said. "Rayna told me about you. She said something about how I wouldn't be able to believe it when I met you."

He raised his eyebrows. "Yeah?"

"Well, no offense, bro, but you don't seem that amazing."

"You're not so mind boggling, either."

"Really?" I started to form a ball of Ice to prove him wrong but Rayna yelled at me.

She walked forward and put her arms around both of our shoulders.

"Well, I can see you guys are getting off to a great start." She turned to me. "Jimmy, we call him that because he can be in two places at once. Sometimes more."

"Yeah," Half said, "I'd like to see you try that one."

"I'd like to see you move a thousand stone blocks with your mind and some frozen water."

"You guys, please!" said Miyoko. "Grow up."

Half hit me on the shoulder. "I'm just playing with you, my man. I'm here to help you."

"You must be on my side, or the Shield wouldn't let you do that." I rubbed my shoulder. "So, what in the world does that mean—you can be in two places at once?"

He shrugged his shoulders. "It's hard to explain. My body can be in two different locations at the same time, each half functioning independently of the other yet aware of what the other is doing at all times. Kind of like magical cloning with a centralized brain. It's probably too much for a boy of your lesser intellect." His smile lessened the insult.

"Wait a minute," I said, baffled. "If you can do that, really be in two places at the same time, then shouldn't you be called Twice instead of Half?"

A look of puzzlement crossed his face, but then his smile returned.

"Oh. Yeah. Okay, so I'm not that good with nicknames. Cut me some slack, man. I was thinking along the lines of splitting myself into two, and one half of me being in each place."

"Whatever," I said. "This could possibly be the weirdest conversation I've had in a long time. So let me see you do it."

"I already am."

"You are? Where's your other . . . half?"

"Watching over your family. See? Maybe you should be nicer to me."

The proverbial light bulb went off in my head.

"What? You mean . . . it was you? Were you peeking in our room a couple of nights ago?"

"Yeah, I noticed you'd been up real late, and I saw your brother get up and act all scared, so I climbed up to see if you were okay."

I couldn't believe my ears. This was so bizarre, I thought.

"So . . . how long have you been doing this?"

"From the beginning, little man." He hit me on the shoulder again. "Where do you think I got that Braves hat?"

"What? You've gotta be kidding me."

"Rayna sent me after you—well, one of me—and the other me stayed behind to let her know what was going on. I was just about to interfere with Dontae the hairy gorilla when your dad showed up to save you. I went and got your hat just for the heck of it."

This was just way too weird. "How do you send . . . the other you places? Do you have something like the Bender Ring?"

"No. I just go. I can't explain it, but I do it. And I can actually be in more than two places if I need to be. The most I've ever been able to replicate of myself is seven."

My head was getting dizzy trying to comprehend his ability. "So where have you been since then? Why haven't we met before?"

For the first time, his eyes dropped and the smile vanished. "I was trying to gather the rest of the Alliance."

I looked over at Rayna, and saw the same expression on her face as the Half's. From what I heard back in the cavern, I knew something terrible had happened, and I was scared to ask. But I did.

"Rayna? Miyoko? What happened?"

"They're all dead, Jimmy," Miyoko answered. "All of them, even the one you call Geezer. They're all . . ." She broke down and sobbed into her dad's shoulder. Tanaka was unusually silent, not having said much since I first helped them all down from the tree.

"Tanaka," I said, "what's wrong with you? I mean, besides the obvious crud that's going on."

"I just worry, Jimmy-san. I just worry. Still no sign of *okisaru* since they chase away Shadow Ka. My daughter's heart broken. Many friends dead. Don't really feel like talking."

Things had to be bad for him to be so sullen, I thought.

"Last question, I promise. Rayna, how did you guys end up in the tree?"

"Ask the Half." She pointed at her badly nicknamed friend.

He threw his arms up in the air. "It's not my fault. I didn't know I had Shadow Ka trailing me."

"After the *okisaru* chased away the Ka from the caves, Half showed up out of the blue. Before we knew it, several Ka jumped us, morphed into humans, tied us up with rope and hoisted us into the tree. They said something about it being a sign for you, to tell you that they'd gone back to join their brothers. Then they turned back into Ka, took flight, and disappeared."

"Why didn't they kill you?" I asked. It was a terrible question.

"Sorry to disappoint you," said Rayna. "I guess the message was more powerful that way. What did they mean, anyway?"

I told them about the Ka that had supposedly abandoned their wicked ways and come back to being real humans. It hadn't lasted very long by the looks of it. I could only hope that at least one of them stayed true, and would go back to help their families like they had promised.

"Something about that makes me very sick inside," said Miyoko.

"At least we know it's possible," I said. "That gives us some hope. My dad did it, those people did it for a while. Maybe some of them did stay clean." I breathed out a huge sigh. "You know, enough with the depressing talk. We've gotta find some food, and I need to sleep for about three days."

The others nodded in agreement, although we had no idea where we would go. We were just beginning to head for the road when a blur of movement behind some trees caught our attention. It was the Bender Ring appearing out of nowhere and falling to the ground, leaving Hood in its wake. He was back.

"Hood," I said, "why are you always running off when it gets dangerous?" I forced out a laugh to show I was joking, but no one else joined in. Miyoko even groaned.

Hood grabbed his ring and ran over to me. There was an obvious sense of urgency in the way he was moving.

"What's wrong, Hooded One?" asked Tanaka.

Hood was looking around frantically for a place to paint some words. He saw a big rock and ran over to it, robe flopping back and forth with every step.

"JIMMY, TIME IS UP. WE MUST GO NOW!"

"Go now? What are you . . ." But I knew exactly what he was talking about, and it hit me way before he finished writing his next words.

"THE LADY FROM YOUR DREAMS. WE HAVE TO GO RIGHT NOW."

What an idiot you are, Jimmy, I thought. How could that have slipped my mind so easily, when she'd made it clear how important it was that I be there? My spirits wilted knowing I couldn't rest for even an hour or two.

But there was no choice. I just hoped she had some food.

"Okay," I said, thinking. The leather case with the Disk still hung by my side, and that was all I needed. "Look, Hood will take me there, and then come back and take all of you to my family in South Carolina. Man, I hope they're still okay."

"Don't worry," said Half. "Right now they're sitting on the porch wondering about you. I'm looking at them with my other half."

I stared at him. Could this guy possibly be for real?

"Are you serious?" I asked.

"Yes, Jimmy, trust me. I think it's time I introduced myself to them. See ya."

He disappeared. No smoke, no noise, nothing. Just like that, he was gone. I looked at Rayna, the shock evident on my face.

"Give me a break," she said. "You've seen a lot weirder stuff than that. Now, I don't know what you're talking about or where you're going, but it looks like you better get on with it. Hood can fill us in when he gets back."

She was right. I walked over and gave her a hug and then did the same with Miyoko and Tanaka.

"Don't worry, old boy," I said to him. "They'll be back. Those *okisaru* are tough little cookies."

"I hope you're right, Jimmy-san. You'll need my army soon, *neh?*"

I nodded and then patted him on the back. Hood grabbed me by the arm and dragged me over to an open spot, sick of my lollygagging. Without hesitating, he raised the Bender Ring over our heads and let it drop.

Soon I was in New York City.

CHAPTER 26

The Big Apple

Hood took us to the exact place he'd seen in a photograph: on the very top of the Empire State Building, on the west side, right next to the viewing window. The glass went up in a flat plane and then curved toward the center of the building, several feet over our heads. I guess the makers of the building frowned upon people jumping off of their investment.

As Hood bent over to pick up the Bender Ring, I took in the remarkable surroundings. It was impossible to tell what time it was, although I thought it was early morning. But the sky was dark with the taint of the Shadow Ka—worse than I'd ever seen it. Never in my life had I even seen a storm that looked so black, and I had been through some doozies living in the tornado-plagued South my whole life.

A mile or two from where we stood, the sky grew even blacker in a big swath across the sky. Where the taint above us looked like a dark, dark gray, the long rent in the sky was the complete absence of light—perfect blackness. A shudder of horror went through my skin, because I knew what it was. And something about it felt very permanent.

It was a Ripping of the Black Curtain. We stared for several minutes, expecting, or at least hoping, that it would seal itself. But it stayed, floating over the earth like a mother spaceship.

And things were coming out of it. Wispy, shapeless things, like ghosts.

"Holy crud, Hood," I said. "Things are worse than we thought."

He nodded his head, looking out into the distance with hooded eyes.

"What is that?" I asked. "Are those things the Stompers?"

Hood knelt down to write on the concrete roof of the building. The clouded darkness made it hard to see, but I could read his words just fine. And they gave me the heebie-jeebies.

"YES, I THINK SO. THE CURTAIN IS BREACHED ONCE AND FOR ALL. TIME IS OUT."

"So those ghost-looking things just fly down and enter our brains? That's how it works?"

"SOMETHING LIKE THAT. I WILL GO NOW."

So much for a long conversation.

"Okay," I said. "Come back for me in a couple of hours. If I'm not here, then come back every two hours after that. Does that work?"

Hood nodded. "I WILL GO AND GATHER EVERYONE ELSE TO YOUR UNCLE'S HOME."

"Sounds good. I just hope that Floating Lady shows up. Is it time yet?"

Hood nodded again and then readied himself to go. A few seconds later he dropped the Ring and was gone.

I was alone, standing on the most famous skyscraper in the world, watching our mortal enemy enter my world just a couple of miles away.

Man, my life was weird.

I sat and stared for quite a while at the surreal scene of the Rip in the Black Curtain, almost hypnotized by it. It was so hard to imagine what the Stompers actually *were*, to visualize and conceptualize what we were dealing with.

What could be more vague than describing them as nightmares?

A tap on my shoulder interrupted my thoughts. *Finally,* I thought as I turned to face the newcomer.

But it wasn't the Floating Lady.

CHAPTER 27
Floating Lady's Digs

It was The Half standing there.

"What are you doing here?" I asked.

"Everyone's safe and happy back at the farm, so I thought I'd come and say howdy. In fact, I'm talking to you and to your mom at the same time. She says hi."

"Ya know, Half, you're really strange."

"Thank you." He turned and jaunted over to the wall by the elevator and plopped down into a sitting position, with his elbows on his knees. "So, where's that lady chick you were supposed to meet?"

"I don't know. She probably wouldn't like you calling her a 'lady chick,' though."

"No, I don't mind."

The woman's voice came from my right, and a quick look revealed the lady from my dream. She wore different clothes, but they were still nondescript and boring. Her hair was frumpy, and her face was lined with worry. Baffled at how she'd managed to sneak up on us, I couldn't think of anything to say.

"But," she continued, "I am sorry, He Who Is Known as The Half. But you must leave, and you must leave now."

"I was just starting to have fun," he countered, but his face revealed that he knew he wouldn't win this argument.

"Go, now," the lady said. "The fate of this world is hanging in the balance. Don't mess it up."

"Man, that's some fancy talk. Fine, see ya." He vanished without another word of complaint.

I turned to the Floating Lady. "I still don't get how he does that."

"Don't worry, much will become clear before you leave me today. Did you bring the Red Disk?"

I patted the leather pack hanging from my neck and shoulder in acknowledgement. "Why did we have to meet here?" I asked.

"Something special waits inside. Also, I wanted you to see the main breach of the Black Curtain. I wanted you to realize that everything must end, for good or for bad, very soon."

"Those things flying out of the Blackness—are those the Stompers?"

"Barely. But yes, that is what they look like before they gain their full power inside the minds of your people. They are worthless and weak until then, until you are prepared and ready in the Coma. That is why they need the Shadow Ka."

"It's all so hard to believe."

"Believe it, Jimmy. Within hours, you will be the last one awake." She said it the same way I'd expect someone to tell me the time.

"Come," she said, motioning to a door. "We have much to discuss."

We walked down a few sets of stairs and through a long, dark hallway. We went through another nondescript door and entered a sparsely furnished apartment. It smelled of scented candles and recently burnt food. The walls were white, and only a picture or two adorned them. There was one lamp in sight, letting out a dull glow at the moment. She had me sit on a brown couch, and then disappeared for a minute. When she came back, she was holding two glasses of water.

I took mine and drank the whole thing in one long gulp.

"Do you have any food?" I felt stupid, but I was starving.

"Yes." She left again and returned with several sandwiches. "Can we finally begin?"

I nodded as I wolfed down one of the PB and Js. It was the best thing I'd ever tasted.

"We have you, we have me, and we have the Red Disk," she said. "Let's begin."

She started talking, and in the next minutes and hours, my world was changed forever all over again.

CHAPTER 28

Inori

"Jimmy," she said, "You have been through three of the Doors. Each time, you were sent to exotic locations, given great riddles to solve, dangerous tasks to achieve. Everything you have done to this day has been a test, everything. My dear boy, I'm proud to say that you have passed those tests, exceeding even the loftiest of our expectations."

"*Our?*" I asked. "You still haven't told me who you are. I don't even know your name for crying out loud."

"I told you, I am a messenger. That's all you need to know."

"Well, I'm sick of calling you the Floating Lady."

She smiled. "My name is Inori. Now let's move on."

"Okay, *Inori.*"

"There is much to accomplish in a short period of time. First, we must get you through the Fourth Door, and to do that, we must have you solve the Riddle of the Red Disk. Once solved, you'll be able to find the Dream Warden, and get the Fourth Gift. It's all quite simple."

"Yeah, I wish it was more complicated, just for fun. Where is the Door anyway?"

"It's right there, silly." She pointed to the front door of her apartment.

"Very funny."

"I'm not joking."

I rolled my eyes. "We just walked through that door. You're telling me the Fourth Gift is out in the hallway?"

"Haven't you learned how this place works? Don't you remember the Door in the Tower of Air? They are not ordinary doors. My, my, my, we have so much to do. Now be quiet and listen to me, okay?"

I nodded, already confused even though she hadn't told me anything yet.

"Now," she continued, clapping her hands together. "Take out the Red Disk."

I pulled the leather carrying case into my lap, unzipped it, and pulled out the disk. Its blood red color and heavy feel reminded me of the Storm World lady that had given it to me. Of all the places I'd been, that had probably been the strangest.

I turned the disk over and over in my hands. It was the size of a normal dinner plate but two or three inches thick. And it was heavier than it looked, five or six pounds. The surface was smooth and shiny, like the hood of a brand new sports car.

"Here it is," I said. "Are you sure your name's not Erifani Tup?"

"There you go again, thinking that's a person. No one ever said that."

"I was told that Erifani Tup would help me figure out how to use the Red Disk. Sure sounds like a person to me— especially considering all the weird names being thrown around since all of this started."

"Well, it is *not* a person. All you were told is that you

needed Erifani Tup to reveal the Red Disk, and you needed the Red Disk to reveal Erifani Tup. That's why it's a riddle."

I threw the disk up in the air and then caught it. Inori gasped.

"Be careful," she said.

"It all sounds like a vicious cycle to me," I said. "I need one for the other, but I need the other for the one."

"Exactly!" she said, more excited than I'd ever seen her. "Now figure it out."

"But . . ."

"No, Jimmy. You've come too far to play the denial game. Suck it up and do it. By the way, I can't help you. You have to do this, one last time."

She was right. I needed to quit dinking around and get to work. I leaned back on the couch and looked at the disk. I turned it over and over and over, trying to think about the riddle. Nothing was popping up in the old noggin.

I closed my eyes, took a deep breath. I felt pretty good now that I'd eaten and had a chance to sit down. I pushed all other thoughts and worries as far away as possible, and turned every ounce of the Jimmy brain onto the problem at hand.

Two words, Erifani Tup.

Not a person. Just words.

A place? No.

A thing? No.

Some kind of magical words, a spell or something? No.

What could it be? I decided to switch my thoughts over to the disk.

A red disk, round and smooth. No discernible features. I needed it to figure out what Erifani Tup . . . was? What it meant? Was the disk some kind of device or tool?

Something was starting to click.

Erifani Tup. It was a clue, a code, some kind of hidden meaning. It was the key to understanding what the Red Disk was used for. And the Red Disk helped you figure out the code, or hidden meaning, of the words Erifani Tup.

What could manipulate words, change them somehow so you could understand their true meaning? My brain strained, reached, searched for the answer that was somewhere out there. And then, like turning on the windshield wipers after idling in the heavy rain, everything became clear.

CHAPTER 29

Erifani Tup

I jumped up. "Inori, do you have a black marker or something, and some paper?"

"Uh . . . yes, yes, of course I do. Hold on."

She ran into the back room and came out with exactly what I'd asked for. She also had a huge smile on her face, and I knew that she knew that I'd figure it out.

I grabbed the marker and paper from her and began scribbling in huge letters across the entire face of it.

"Where's the bathroom?" I asked.

"This way."

I followed her into the hallway and through a small door. She flipped the switch, and I held the piece of paper up against my chest and turned to the mirror.

Although most of the letters were backward, it read as easily as saying ABC.

ꟼUT IИAꟻIЯƎ

Now I knew exactly what the Red Disk was. It was a mirror, and it needed to be burned in order to use it.

Which left only one question. Why in the world did I need a mirror?

"Do you have a fireplace?" I asked her, anxious and excited.

"Follow me." She led me out of the bathroom and back into the main entry with the old brown couch. We went from there into the kitchen, where she had disappeared to make the sandwiches. It looked like something from an old museum—forty- or fifty-year-old appliances, terrible yellow patterned countertops, and a big thing with a handle on it that looked like a torture device.

But the object that stood out the most was an old fashioned stove made of iron, with a swinging, grated door inside of which a hot fire was burning. A pipe led up from the stove and disappeared into the ceiling. It seemed very out of place.

"What is that thing doing here?" I asked. "Inside a huge skyscraper?"

"Because I can have anything I want here—something you will understand later."

"What does that mean?"

"Don't worry about it." She grabbed a pot holder and opened the door of the stove. "Go on, throw it in."

I looked at the disk, thinking it through one last time. I had to be right, especially considering the way Inori was acting. If I was wrong, she would've been much more hesitant to show me a fire.

I got a firm, two-handed grip on the disk, bent over toward the hot flames, and tossed it in.

The fire flared into a brilliant white burst of flame, like someone had thrown in a bucket of gasoline. I strained to see the disk and what was happening to it. The heat made it impossible to get too close, and the licking tendrils of the fire hid it from my view. I waited a few more minutes, hoping Inori would offer some insight.

When she didn't, I said, "So when and how do we get it out?"

Inori walked over to a cabinet, opened it, and pulled out a long iron tool that had a handle on one end and rounded claspers on the other.

"Use this," she said.

I took it from her and tested the handle. When I pulled its lever down, the claspers came together with a snap. It looked like it would cut someone's fingers right off.

I grabbed the handle with two hands and put the other end into the fire. I felt around until the tool knocked on something hard and firm. I moved it around until my senses told me that it was in position, and then I pulled down on the lever. But when I pulled it out, there was nothing on the other end.

"You know what, I'm being an idiot," I said.

"What do you mean?"

"All I have to do is reach in there and grab it—the Shield will protect me."

"Even your hands?"

"Sure. Worst-case scenario is it won't let me touch it."

I reached my hand forward like a man trying to pet a vicious dog, scared of its bite. Shield or no Shield, it just felt wrong to put your hand into a roaring fire. But the Shield repelled the heat and flame as I got closer and closer. Soon I was past the lining of the door and inside the stove. My hand felt nothing but air.

I felt around and found the Red Disk. It was cool to the touch, and I didn't know if that was the Shield or just some new magic in my life. I gripped the Disk and pulled it out of the stove. It almost slipped out of my one hand but I caught it with the other just in time. I straightened to a standing position, and held out the disk so that Inori and I could both see it well.

The Red Disk was no longer red.

It was a perfectly circular, two-inch-thick mirror—not blackened or charred like it had just come out of a hot fire. I could see the ceiling and light fixture reflected back at me. Inori said nothing, and after a few seconds I held the mirror up to look at myself.

Except I wasn't there. Everything else behind me was reflected in perfect form—the refrigerator, the cabinets, the horrible wallpaper. But not me.

My face was nowhere to be seen.

CHAPTER 30

Mirror, Mirror

"What in the world?" I said. Looking in a mirror and not seeing yourself was an odd sensation. I moved it around at different angles, but I never showed up. Everything else in the reflection moved just as my instincts would've expected, but there was no Jimmy Fincher.

"What is this?" I asked Inori. "Am I a vampire or something?" I saw a movie once that taught me the old myth that vampires can't be seen in mirrors. Then I had another creepy thought. The Sounding Rod had also not shown its reflection. What was going on?

"Have you forgotten the purpose of the Disk?" she replied.

I walked around behind her and then held the Disk up in a way that I would see Inori's reflection in the mirror. But there was no sign of her, either.

"All I remember is that it was supposed to help me find the Dream Warden," I said.

"Exactly."

"You mean . . ."

"Yes. Only the Dream Warden will show his or her face in

this mirror. That is how you will know, and there will be no doubt."

"Well, it's obviously not you. No offense."

"Offense? You think I would *want* that duty? No thanks."

"What does that mean, anyway? What is the Dream Warden? Can he destroy the Stompers or something?"

"You'll find out when you go through the fourth and final Door. The trials are all over now. It's time to fight."

She turned and walked out of the kitchen. I looked at the mirror once more and then hurried after her. I went into the main room and saw her sitting on the couch. She caught my eye and then pointed to the front door. It had changed.

Minutes before it had been a plain white door typical of an apartment complex. Now it was brown wood, ancient and scarred, with worn-down carvings and curvy edges. It looked just like the others.

So this is the last one, I thought.

"It's ready when you are," said Inori. "But first, we need to talk. Have a seat."

I sat down next to her and waited for her to begin. She took the mirror from me and helped put it back in my leather case, which she then slipped onto my shoulders.

"Take that with you, you'll need it when the time comes." She cleared her throat.

"Now, listen very carefully. I need to tell you more about the Yumeka, the World of Dreams. I know we've already discussed some of this, but it's so important, we need to revisit the subject.

"There is a big difference between *dreaming,* and entering the Yumeka. They are not the same. Not at all. The Yumeka is more of an extension of our own waking world, a union of dreams with real life. It's so hard to understand, and even more difficult to explain. But the key is this—you must never underestimate what it is to be in Yumeka. If you look at it as having a hunky-dory dream, you will never survive."

I tried to think of a question to ask while she paused, but nothing popped in my head. This made me realize how clueless I truly was.

"You must look at it as a *place,*" she continued, "not a figment of imagination or thought. When I came to you the first time, you were having a normal dream—a series of images in your subconscious mind. Why you were hanging from a rope and all that I have no idea—you're a strange kid." I started to protest, but she held her hand up. "But anyway, I pulled you out of that and into the Yumeka. It can be done— the Stompers do not own it, they only rule it. And they rule it with a terror which I need not speak of.

"I think you felt the difference that day."

I nodded. I remembered the transition—somehow I had known that I was no longer dreaming in the real sense. Or unreal sense. Or whatever.

"Again, the Yumeka is a place. When you see other people there, you are really seeing them, not dreaming about them. They are seeing you as well. Again, it's difficult to grasp, but I want to stress that point. The Yumeka is a place, it is real, and being there, under the control of the Stompers, is far beyond that which is conveyed by the simple word, nightmare. It is truly *living* those nightmares."

"So how on earth am I supposed to beat the Stompers? I know I can't use the Anything to do it—it won't let me just kill or get rid of them all, will it?"

"You're right. The Anything will serve its purposes in the

end but not for the Stompers themselves. For that you will need the Fourth."

"What is the Fourth Gift anyway?" I asked.

"The answer to that question lies behind the Door, Jimmy. I think you'd better get going, although there is so much to tell. When you come back, if there is time, I will tell you more."

"Wait, one more thing. When you came to me before, you mentioned the Layers—you made it sound extremely important."

"Yes, just when you think it couldn't be any worse, there is always more." She sighed and leaned back into the couch. "The Stompers are never satisfied with your first round of fear. If you fail, Jimmy, they will torment and haunt you until you grow immune to it. Then they will lift you into another Layer of the Yumeka. There, they will subject you to a new life— either a repeat of the old one or perhaps even some new life, with new memories and new friends and family. Maybe even set on a world you didn't come from. Whatever they think will cause you the most fear when they send the Shadow Ka and start the process all over again.

"All the while, the Shadow Ka are taking care of your actual sleeping, physical body, keeping you nourished and strong so they can use you for decades. Layer after Layer, new nightmare after new nightmare, you will live in horror for the rest of your days."

My face had no blood left in it, drained by the terrible things she told me.

"This is all making me sick," I said and stood up. I paced the room back and forth, my stomach twisted and nauseous. "What are they? How can they be so evil?"

"Because the Stompers *are* evil, Jimmy. That is what they

are made of. When the Givers translated their name into our language, they chose *Stompers* because that is what they do. They stomp out every last hope and will to live. They stomp out your every reason to exist. They do it so they can survive in your place."

"Then what are the Givers?"

"They are the opposite of the Stompers, that's all I know. They are good, where the Stompers are evil. Now, you must go."

I looked at her and then down at the floor. My courage was weak, and I didn't want to go anywhere near that door. Half of me wanted to give up and run away.

But I couldn't. I was the only hope.

I thought of my family. I thought of Tanaka, and Rayna, and Miyoko. I thought of the Hooded One and the Half. I thought of all my friends back home.

For them. For them I at least had to try.

I walked up to the Door, pulled it open, and stepped through.

CHAPTER 31

The Farm

When I received the first three Gifts, I'd been underground, in an indoor blizzard, and in the middle of the desert. Now I felt a nervous excitement wondering where this new place would be. I closed the Door behind me as I looked at my new surroundings.

This time I was in an open field of knee-high wheat, stretching in every direction all the way to the horizon, with a blue sky and bright sun overhead. A soft breeze threw waves along the wheat like gentle ocean surf, and the clean smell of fresh air and growing crops filled my nose. There was no break to the endless wheat other than the slightly undulating hills—no trees, no tractors, no animals—except for one very big thing.

To my right stood a huge farmhouse. It was yellow, two stories tall, and had a wraparound porch. Behind it was a barn—the kind every kid played with as part of a toy farm set. It was bright red, with big swinging doors and a four-sided roof. On top was a large iron weather vane shaped like a rooster.

Coming out of the barn, wiping his hands on a dirty towel, was the same man who'd given me so much already.

How perfect a setting for our last meeting, I thought.

It was Farmer, dressed in his usual garb—flannel shirt and overalls. But I was wrong in thinking it would be our last time seeing each other.

"Hello, Jimmy," he said as he walked up to me. "How wonderful to see you again." He turned to the farm and opened his arms wide as if he were embracing it. "What do you think of my place?"

"It's great," I said. "Where are we when we meet, anyway?"

"Oh, it's hard to explain. By now you have heard of the Yumeka, am I right?"

"Yeah. Why haven't you ever told me about that before?"

Farmer sat back onto an invisible chair—a trick I'd seen him do before. "Well, for one thing we've never had much time. The Stompers have always caught up to us, and they probably will today also. For another thing, I needed you to grow and learn a little more so that you would be able to accept it. And to be honest, you're not done learning all that you must know. There are still some hard lessons yet to come, my gifted friend."

Wondering if I could do the same trick, I tested my faith and leaned back and down as if sitting on a chair. I fell flat on my bottom. Farmer laughed.

"Some things about the Yumeka take years of practice," he said.

"We're in the World of Dreams right now?" I asked as I

brushed myself off. "Can you make me one of those chairs, by the way?"

Farmer closed his eyes for just a moment, and then opened them again. "Yes, we are, and yes, you can sit down now."

A little more slowly than last time, I sat down and it worked—my very own magical chair.

"So . . . how . . . I don't get it."

Farmer smiled and crossed his legs. "The Stompers are not the only masters of the Yumeka. Although our power here grows very weak. In the end, they always find us, and we are forced to run."

"How did you survive that ordeal in the desert—the wall of blackness?"

"I was only hanging around that long to help get you out. The second you went through the door, I took myself away."

My brain hurt. "So . . . I still don't get it. When I came through the Door, did I go to sleep or what? How does that work?"

"Ah, one lesson that we must save for last. Don't worry, you will understand the answer to that question after you beat the Stompers."

If I had been eating food, I would've spit it clear across to the barn. "After I beat the Stompers? Are you crazy? You make it sound so easy. I don't even know what to do."

"You will, Jimmy, you will."

"If you say so." I shifted in my chair. "Okay, what's next? I don't quite understand the connection between the Fourth Gift and the Dream Warden. I brought along the Red Disk— well the Used-to-Be Red Disk—but I don't even know who or what the Warden is supposed to be. This mirror is a little freaky by the way."

"I'm not sure what freaky means, but yes, the Disk is an amazing thing, and extremely important. Everything depends on the Warden of Dreams, you know."

"Then why do you need me?"

Farmer laughed. "Why do we need you? You've asked me some silly questions before, but that just might beat them."

"Huh? What do you mean? You just said that everything depended on the Dream Warden."

"It does."

I gave him a blank look.

"Come. Everything will make sense soon."

He stood and began walking back to the barn. I followed. When we got to the entrance, he paused and turned to me.

"To beat the Stompers and end their reign in your world, we will need you *and* the Dream Warden. Not one more than the other, not one less than the other. Come inside."

The barn was dark compared to the bright sun outside. As my eyes adjusted, Farmer led me to a workbench. It was made of wood and came to my chest. Dozens of various tools and tractor parts littered the top of it. Farmer leaned against it, resting on his elbows.

"Based on our prior experiences, we better do this quickly and make sure you leave here with the Fourth Gift."

He reached for a small cloth bag that rested near the back of the bench. It was pulled closed with a drawstring, and Farmer held it out toward me, resting on his palm.

"What yummy stuff do you have in store for me this time?" I asked.

"Open it and see."

I put the bag on the bench and worked the string loose.

Then I poured its contents onto my palm. It was one small green sphere.

A pea.

"Is this your idea of a joke?" I asked.

"Yes," he said. "Now eat it."

CHAPTER 32

Gift Number Four

I popped the pea into my mouth and chewed it quickly. Like the other Gifts, it had no taste, for which I was very grateful. I despised peas the way I despised hammering nails into my skull.

After I'd swallowed, I looked at Farmer. "Now what?" I asked.

"Raise your right arm, Jimmy."

I wanted to complain, having been through this lesson three times before. But I knew better, and did as he said.

"Now raise your left arm."

I did.

"There wasn't really a need for that this time, but I just wanted to see you do it again." He smiled.

"Farmer, you're getting more and more hilarious every time I meet you."

"What do you have, when you have no humor, I say." He let out a huge sigh as he sat back onto one of his special chairs. "Now, to tell you about the Fourth Gift, the last you will receive before the end."

"What is it?" A sudden excitement shot through me, as I remembered Farmer telling me last time that this one would be even more powerful than the Anything, which seemed impossible.

Farmer leaned back further in his invisible chair. His smile faded, and he spoke his next words in a whisper.

"You now have the power to control the Yumeka."

"Control the Yumeka?" I asked. "What . . . what does that mean? I can just go there and wipe out the Stompers?"

"No, it most certainly does *not* mean that. The Stompers are only *inside* the Yumeka, they have nothing to do with it per se. You must still go there and defeat them in the only way you can in such a place."

"And how is that?"

"Using the Fourth Gift. It's called the Power, and it will help you overcome the nightmares."

He stood and leaned forward until his face was only inches from mine.

"You must do it for everyone. For everyone in your world."

His words turned my blood into a flowing red Slurpee.

"That sounds awful," I said.

Farmer sat back down. "Jimmy, please understand that I will joke no more with you today, because we've breached a subject that doesn't allow it. Yes, what you must do is awful. Much more than you can now envision. But you must do it. You are the only hope now, the only one. I hate to do this . . ."

Farmer broke into a sob, and his shoulders shook with grief.

"I feel for you as I would my own son, Jimmy. I detest the Stompers for making me put this burden upon you. But it must be done." He stood again. "Jimmy, I know you can do this. You will win in the end. I feel this in my heart."

My own eyes were wet with fear and sadness. The severity of Farmer's words had punctured my insides, and I knew that I was about to embark on something that I could not yet comprehend.

"How . . . how do I do it?"

"You must allow the Shadow Ka to put you in the Black Coma and fly you to the eye of the Stomper assigned to you. After you defeat your own nightmares, then you'll take on the others."

"And how does that happen?"

"That's where the Dream Warden comes in."

There was a long pause.

"The Warden has a gift of his own," Farmer continued. "By now you have heard of the Grand Exception?"

"Yeah—it's what the girl, the other Giver, did to save Joseph. You can willingly take the place of another, and the Stompers can do nothing about it."

"That's exactly right. Well, the Dream Warden has a special power that allows him to use the Grand Exception an infinite number of times. Through the power of the Warden, you will be able to take the place of every person on your planet, and fight their nightmares for them. And believe me, Jimmy, it is the only way. Those people cannot do it—they don't have the power or the means or the will. You must do it with your Gifts. It's the only way."

It was almost too much to sink in. The power to control the Yumeka, the Grand Exception, the Dream Warden. They all fit together like the sides of a triangle. Before I could say something to Farmer, he stood and looked out the doors.

"We knew this would happen," he said.

"What?"

He turned back to me.

"They are here."

CHAPTER 33

Flee

Farmer grabbed my hand and dragged me out of the barn. A great wind had picked up, and I didn't have to look to see its source. The Stompers had found us, quicker than ever before.

"But I don't know everything yet!" I yelled over the wind. "Where is the Dream Warden? How do I use the Power?"

"We can't chance it!" Farmer yelled back. "You'll figure it out yourself. If we don't get you out now, it's over. Run for the Door, go!"

I didn't want to, but I did what he said. I turned and ran straight for it, pounding the wheat stalks under me with every step. Behind the Door, moving toward us like a black wave, was the wall of the Stompers. Wind tore at my back as the wall tried to suck everything into it. If it got much closer, it would be strong enough to lift me off the ground.

But the Door was close now, and I knew I would make it without the tense moments of the last time I'd met Farmer. I ran the last few steps and grabbed the handle. Just before I pushed it open, I looked back at the old Giver.

He waved, a simple act of lifting his hand and then letting it fall back to his side.

I nodded to him and then went through the Door.

I closed it from the other side, and did a double take. The instant it sealed shut, it transformed back into the plain white door of the apartment. I was surprised to feel a twinge of sadness, knowing that would be my last magical door.

I turned to tell Inori about what happened.

She was sitting on the couch, but she wasn't alone.

Hood was standing next to her, looking at me through his old, dirty robe.

I leaned back against the door. Inori's face was ashen, and her eyes were sullen. Hood's head was drooping.

Something was wrong. Well, *more* wrong than having a whole world taken over by ghostlike Freddy Kruegers.

"Hood, has it really been two hours?"

His pale hand came out of his robes and he held up five fingers.

"Five hours?" It seemed impossible that much time had passed. "Well, what's wrong? Inori, you look terrible."

She nodded her head to the far wall that had the door to the kitchen. It had been the only one in the house with some color—a fading puke green. Now, white painted words were scrawled all over it from top to bottom.

One sentence, right in the middle, stood out like a naked sumo wrestler in a room full of ballerinas.

"THEY HAVE JIMMY'S FAMILY AND WANT TO MAKE A DEAL."

CHAPTER 34

Decision

I didn't want to read the rest, although words like 'kidnapped' and 'last ones' and 'kill' jumped out at me.

"What's going on?" I asked Inori.

"Jimmy." She motioned for me to sit with her. After I plopped down on the couch beside her, she continued.

"I told you we had only a matter of hours before the Stompers' takeover was complete." She paused and stole a glance at Hood. "Well, it's over. Your family and the remaining members of the Alliance are the last ones awake. The Ka have saved them for the end because they want to make a deal with you."

"A deal? What, are they trying to sell me a used car?" I wasn't really trying to make a joke—I was just angry they had the gall to use my family like this.

"According to Hood, they said they would leave your family and Hood and the others free from the Black Coma and the Stompers, forever. All you have to do is promise to stop, and leave them alone."

"That's ridiculous!" I yelled. "What's the point in being

free from the Coma if the rest of the world is dead?" I stood and walked around the room, fuming. I couldn't remember the last time I'd felt so angry. A swelling hatred filled my mind and body as I thought of Rusty and Mom and Dad held by those hideous beasts. Time after time the Ka had taken my loved ones, hoping to use them against me.

And then the awful truth really sunk in. It was working.

I thought of all the time I'd wasted saving my family and friends. One instance after another, I'd put the main quest aside to rescue everyone from the latest and greatest predicament. That was exactly what the Ka wanted—every second they could delay me, the stronger the Stompers grew, the more people fell into their grasp.

And now, it was complete. The whole world had fallen. My circle of family and friends was the last little island yet to be swallowed by an ocean of nightmares and fear.

But . . . no. I couldn't have done it any differently. Farmer even told me once that the reason I was able to get through the Door in the woods in the first place was because of the purity of my intentions. How could I abandon the ones closest to me? How could I do that and still call myself human?

I was determined to prevent this from becoming an either-or situation. I would not, and would never, allow my family to come second. But I would also not allow the Stompers to win.

We were going to win on both fronts.

"Jimmy?" Inori asked. "Are you okay? What are you thinking about?"

I looked at her, snapped out of my thoughts. "I'm just thinking about everything and what we need to do."

"Jimmy, you have the Four Gifts. There *is* only one thing to do. It's time to face the Stompers."

"You don't understand, Inori!" I was yelling, and felt bad for it. But they had to understand. "They're not our only enemy in this war. We have two battles to win."

In that instant, the plan solidified in my mind. Everything came together in a moment of perfect clarity. It would work, and when it was done, the Stompers would still be there and I could deal with them then. I looked at Hood, and then at Inori.

"Jimmy," she said, "you're up to something."

"I know what I have to do," I replied. "And I know that in the end I have to find the Dream Warden and face the Stompers."

I paused and considered my thoughts one last time. And then I decided.

"But first, we're gonna rid this world of every last Shadow Ka."

CHAPTER 35

Gone South

I expected Inori to complain, but she did the opposite.

"You're right, Jimmy. It's just that I thought that part would come after you defeat the Stompers, not before. Every second we delay, their hold upon the minds of all those people grows stronger."

"But think about it," I countered. "The Black Coma is *caused* by the Shadow Ka. If we release people from the Stompers, who's to say the Ka won't just put them right back in the coma, and then invite their masters to return?"

Hood knelt to the wooden floor and wrote two words.

"I AGREE."

Inori thought for a moment. "Okay." She nodded. "But your plan has to work, and it has to work quickly. We can't waste any more time."

"All right then, let's get moving." A thought popped in my head. "Inori, is there any way you can help find the Dream Warden while we deal with the Shadow Ka?"

She laughed. "Oh, you don't need to worry about that part."

"What do you mean?"

"You've already found the Warden of Dreams."

"What?"

"You'll see, you'll see. Let's go."

Confused but knowing we were crunched for time, I forced myself to put that aside until later. I trusted Inori, and it was a relief to see that she wasn't worried about that piece of the puzzle.

And so it was that I found myself scrunched together with a hooded ghost and a lady who made good sandwiches and liked to float around in the air occasionally.

I reread the words "THEY HAVE JIMMY'S FAMILY . . ." as Hood lifted the Bender Ring over our heads and let it drop.

Seconds later we were in the living room of my uncle's house.

We had barely stepped away from the Ring before Miyoko and Rayna smothered me with hugs. I was so glad to see them, I squeezed right back. Then Joseph smothered me as well.

"Fill me in," I said after we let go. Tanaka was also there, as was Justin, the Half.

"They have your family," said Miyoko, "but left the rest of us to make sure you got their message nice and clear."

"Where are they?"

"They're out in the fields," said Joseph. "There are probably a hundred of those suckers, closely guarding your family. We considered attempting a rescue but thought better of it. We didn't want to take any chances until you got here."

"Thanks. By the way, this is Inori." I pointed to her. "She

won't really tell me where she came from, but I think she's an outcast member of the Alliance."

"I'm on your side, that's all that matters," she said.

"Tanaka," I said, and gave him a hug, too. For once, his smell didn't make my nose beg for relief. "Jeez, did you shower or something?"

"Rayna made me." His frown showed he didn't like it too much.

"Wow, I can actually see the separate hairs of your hanging eyebrows. I thought they were sealed together forever with grease."

"You very hilarious," he said.

"Hey, did the *okisaru* ever come back?"

"Yes, Jimmy-san. They are here, ready to fight for you."

"Good, we'll need them. You know, Tanaka, I think I liked you better before you got so serious. Make a joke once in a while, would ya?"

"I not so funny looking after you get here," he replied.

"I have no idea what you meant by that," I said, "but at least you tried."

Half came up, holding the Braves hat he'd left for us earlier.

"I'm offended, Jimmy. I go through all that trouble to get this back to you, and you haven't even put it on your head yet."

"The water shrunk it. Sorry."

"I think your head's just gotten bigger with all your fancy Gifts." He flipped the hat over onto the couch. "So did you ever figure out the Red Disk?"

"Yeah, I'll show it to you guys later, but let's get my family back first."

"I can tell you've already got something up your sleeve," said Rayna.

"You're right, I do. All I need are three things to get started."

"What's that?" asked Miyoko.

"The Anything, the *okisaru,* and a whole lot of courage."

CHAPTER 36

So, We Meet Again

We spent the next thirty minutes developing and perfecting my plan. At first the others thought it was way too far-fetched, but I was able to convince them that it was the best way. The biggest doubt I had was something about the *okisaru,* but Tanaka assured me that they could turn into *anything.*

And so it was set. Now everything just had to run without a hitch.

"Inori, I'm sorry you don't have a part in the plan. I didn't really think you would end up coming with us. I thought you would be like Farmer and just disappear."

She laughed. "I'm not a Giver, Jimmy, although I'm more like them than you might imagine. No, I'm like the Alliance—different like them."

Something about her words didn't compute.

"What do you mean, different? You have a Gift?"

"No, not really. It's just another one of those things that you'll find out later."

I shrugged. "Whatever. Anyway, I don't think you should

come out there with us—it's too dangerous. Should I have Hood take you back to New York?"

"No, I don't need that. Just go. I'll be fine, I promise you. Actually . . ."

"What?"

"I would like some sort of protection. Could you leave the Half with me?"

"Half? What, do you have a crush on him or something?"

Half spoke up. "There's no way I don't go out there. I'm fighting."

"Please!" yelled Inori. Then she calmed her face. "I'm sorry. I just . . . the thought of being left alone just scares me, that's all. I'm too important, Jimmy, I need someone here to protect me."

I studied her face, trying to see if she was hiding something. Well, I knew she was hiding something, but I wanted to know if it was worth my time to grill it out of her. I decided it wasn't.

"All right, then. Half, you stay." He started to protest, but I held my hand up. "Please, Half. She's right—it's as important we keep her safe as it is we get rid of the Ka."

"Fine." He went over and sat down on the couch. "But if you do have a crush on me," he looked at Inori, "let's get one thing straight. I don't go for older women."

She laughed, and Half tried his best not to smile but did anyway.

"Glad we got that settled. We'll see you guys back in here when we're . . . done. Inori, I think I'm going to need your help before I go to meet the Stompers. Which reminds me, will you hold onto this until I get back?" I handed her my leather case.

"Yes, I think you will need my help, and yes, I will hold

that for you." She reached out and grabbed the pack then shook my hand. "Good luck."

"You sound like I'm going to play in a basketball game or something."

"Okay, fine. May the graces of God be with you on the battlefield. Better?"

"Now you sound like a bad movie. See ya soon." I turned to the others. "Let's go."

We filed out of the house, the smallest army in history. Rayna, Miyoko, the Hooded One, Tanaka and his *okisaru,* Joseph, and myself. The sun was just beginning its trip down to the far horizon—it would be dark within a couple of hours. The thought sent a chill down my spine—by the time the sun set, all of this would probably be over.

And then the real terror would start.

The cool air was refreshing, and the smell of grass and bark and other nature-type things filled my nostrils. In another time, the feel of being outside on a day like that would've been such a thrill, and I would've searched the house top to bottom to find a football to toss around.

But these were darker times, and my only hope was that someday soon everything could be back to normal.

Far out in the field, there was a gathering of black shapes, huddled together in a mass of bodies, protecting something in the middle. They had my family. How easy it would be for me to just walk out there and grab them, I thought. But not this time. Today we were going to accomplish a much greater task than just saving my brother and parents.

From my right a swarm of butterflies appeared out of nowhere, having flown in from wherever they'd been waiting for their next assignment. I didn't know much about how they thought, but I knew they were in for a big surprise today. Tanaka walked over to them and they hovered around him. He began to whisper, telling them our plan.

The others stood next to me, peering out into the fields.

A lone shape lifted out of the pack of Ka and flew toward us. Its black wings beat the air as it approached, making that familiar sound of laundry flapping in the wind as it hung out to dry.

When the Ka neared twenty feet from where we stood, it dropped to the ground. Folding its wings back into their resting position, the Ka walked up to within a few feet of us. The sloshing, sucking sound started, and the Shadow Ka began its morphing. Over the next few seconds we witnessed the reverse evolution as the black receded and the human shape took form.

It finished, and I noticed that its eyes remained pitch black, solid orbs of darkness with no whites to be seen. His human form looked old and frail, with shoulders slightly hunched over. The skin on his face was wrinkled and yellow. I knew that face, and I wasn't the least bit surprised when I saw it.

Most knew him as a man named Custer Bleak.

But I had always called him Raspy.

CHAPTER 37

No Deal

"I knew it would be you," I said. "How fitting."

"Of course, Jimmy," he replied.

His voice had been the reason for the name I'd given him. It was scratchy and cruel, filled with phlegm and malice. I hated his voice almost as much as I hated what he'd become. He was by every definition a monster.

"Who else would I send to do my business? There are others you may know as well."

His mouth opened wide, and a scream burst out of it that made me flinch. It seemed impossible that the creature standing there could create such a sound.

Two more Ka flew out of the distant pack and headed our way. A minute later they were standing behind Raspy, fully morphed back into humans. And Custer was right, I knew them well.

The tall one I called Monster, and the other Hairy, for reasons obvious to everyone standing with me.

I had kicked both of them in the past, giving one a broken nose and the other a nice fall, out of a speeding boat. Thinking back on it gave me a small sense of satisfaction. It also made me realize how much I'd changed since we'd last met. I felt like a completely different person. Some people would say that I had become a man.

"The Bumbling Duo. Good to see you again. How's the nose, big guy?" I nodded my head toward Monster.

"There comes a day," he replied, "when you will never smile again. Enjoy it while you can."

I turned to Hairy, otherwise known as Dontae. "I see turning into a Shadow Ka hasn't helped your problem at all. Do women Ka like hairy backs as much as your gorilla kin?"

Hairy said nothing but gave me a nasty look.

"Enough," said Raspy. "I see you are still the little brat that the Mayor brought to me months ago. How simply wonderful that the fate of your world lies on the shoulders of such an incompetent boob."

With a quick thought I formed circles of hard Ice around each of their necks, and then shrunk them—squeezing the breath out of them. All three of them struggled, grabbing the Ice collars with both hands. I snapped my fingers and the Ice vanished into the air.

"Careful what you say, old man. Show me respect, or I'll end this right now."

Raspy tried to recover, but I could tell that I had gotten to him.

"You don't scare me, boy," he said, his shaky voice revealing quite the opposite. "Do whatever you want to me, but if you want to save your family, you'd better listen."

"Go ahead, I can't wait."

"You know that eventually you will lose. You can fight us all you want, but you must meet the Stompers soon, and at that time your family *will* be taken into the Black Coma. You know this. There is nothing you can do—there are too many Ka in this world for you to fight."

"That's debatable, but what's your point?"

"We offer a truce. You, your family, this . . . *Alliance*. Free forever from the grip of the Stompers in exchange for your death."

"My *death?*"

"Yes, it's the only way we can know you will keep your word. If we leave you alive, you will just come back again to haunt us. Your death, in exchange for the lives of those you love."

I laughed, an actual, genuine laugh. "Talk about the pot calling the kettle black. You expect me to believe that you'll leave my family alone after I'm dead?"

"You can watch while we give them over to the Givers. Then you'll know of their safety. We can't really . . . touch the Givers." He said the last part like it had been a frustration for centuries.

"Raspy, I think you're scared. This seems too desperate, even for you."

"I will pander no longer with you!" he screamed, his voice laced with insanity. "We made a deal before, and it saved your father! Now choose again!"

"*Saved* my father?" I couldn't believe this man. "Are you really that crazy? Do you really think I'm that stupid?"

"You will not talk to—"

"BE QUIET!" I yelled at the top of my lungs. In the same instant I formed Ice inside his mouth, choking off his words and making him gag. After several seconds, I released it.

"We're done hearing your lunatic words. Leave. There's

no deal except this—any Ka who wants to change, to come back and leave your evil behind, can be saved. But they better decide quickly, because we're coming for them."

"Then no deal indeed," he said, spitting on the ground. "Your pride will cause your family to live in eternal fear."

With a quick flash of black, the three formed back into Shadow Ka. They extended their wings and lifted into the air. Soon they were gone, back with the rest of them out in the fields.

"I can't believe that guy," I said to the others. "Are we ready?"

"Ready," said Rayna.

"Ready," said Miyoko.

"Ready, boss," said Joseph.

Hood tapped me on the shoulder to indicate his reply.

"Tanaka?" I asked. "Are you and the *okisaru* ready?"

"Aye, aye, captain," he replied.

"Tanaka, please don't ever say that again." I winked at him, and then smiled at the others. I wanted them all to think that I was full of confidence, although deep down I was scared to pieces. "Well, I guess we're ready then."

I turned back to face the Ka out in the fields. It was time for the first part of our plan.

I closed my eyes and called upon the Anything.

CHAPTER 38

Gathering

Farmer had made sure I understood that I could only use my Third Gift four times. This would be my third chance. I'd wanted to use it so many times since I'd eaten those four beans the Giver gave me. But they were too important, and I knew we would need them in the end, especially the very last one.

The other instruction had been that the Anything couldn't be used to maim or kill another living being. Otherwise I would've just destroyed the Ka and the Stompers a long time ago. But it had finally hit me in Inori's apartment how I could use it and still follow the rules.

Throwing all my thoughts into the powerful Third Gift, I reached out with my mind and told the Anything to bring every Shadow Ka in our world, every one, no exceptions, to the endless fields in front of me. I commanded it to use all of its power to gather them here, so that all could be decided in one last battle, here and now, once and for all.

I added one last request into my third using of the Gift. Since it would bring evil creatures from all over the world to

153

me, I thought it could handle just one more. One that wasn't evil at all.

I commanded the Third Anything to bring me a horse. A specific horse.

Baka.

After I opened my eyes, everything was silent for a long few minutes. My companions shifted back and forth on their feet, and the Shadow Ka in the distance appeared restless. And then things changed.

It started as a slight breeze and then picked up to a steady bluster. It was the only sound I could hear, and reminded me of the spooky, blowing wind you always hear in scary movies as the person who's about to be killed walks down a dark alley.

And then it turned into a hurricane.

From all directions the sky darkened—far more than the taint of the Ka that had already been there. Shifting shapes caused the growing shadow, flying in the air toward the fields in front of us. It looked like the atmosphere was disappearing and outer space itself was devouring the sky, a shrinking hole with us at the center.

The Anything was granting my wish.

Soon we could make out the actual shapes of the thousands of Shadow Ka. They were not flying of their own accord— in fact, they were doing everything in their power to beat the invisible force and fly the other direction. But it was too powerful. Ka after Ka plummeted to the ground and landed in the fields behind Raspy and the others. Their fall slowed just before they hit so they were not injured.

More and more came. As they collected in a great mass, the

greens and yellows and browns of the farmland were replaced with blackness, growing outward like a great plague. It went on for some time. Soon they stretched out before us like a black sea, and we could no longer tell where it ended.

And then it stopped. The vast army of Ka, shell-shocked and angry, looked at us as one, ready to unleash their fury on whomever had caused their unplanned trip.

"Jimmy!" yelled Miyoko. "Look! To the north!"

I glanced that way, and saw a new object heading straight for me. As its size grew with its approach from the sky, I could make out four legs and a very long face.

I couldn't imagine what had just gone through poor Baka's head as he flew across half the world.

He landed with a soft thump and then nickered. He looked healthy enough, so all the food we left him must have been enough. His panic was obvious, but when he saw me, a calm went over him and he trotted up to where I stood. Then he nuzzled my shoulder with his nose.

"Howdy, Baka," I said. "You didn't think I'd go off to war without you, right? I need someone to ride into battle." I patted his head and then walked down his length, trying to soothe him with a soft rub.

"Rayna, will you help me get on this guy?"

She nodded, walked over, and put her hands together for me to step on. I put my foot into her cupped fingers and she boosted me up until I could swing my leg over Baka. He had no saddle of course, but I'd ridden bareback before.

"Tanaka, let's do it."

He yelled out a command, and the butterflies swarmed away from him. They spread out until we were surrounded, and bright lights flashed everywhere.

The *okisaru* did their thing, changing into what we wanted for the first phase of battle.

Soon we had an entire army of horses at our disposal.

CHAPTER 39

A Sword of Ice

Every last *okisaru* had changed into a tall, muscled, powerful horse. They spread out across the yard like the full cavalry of King Arthur, lined up and ready for battle. Some were brown, some were black, and others were white. But they all were strong, and their eyes looked ahead at the Shadow Ka with a fierceness that even Rayna couldn't match. Tanaka had never been able to take a full count of how many of these magical creatures were at his command, but we knew there were at least a thousand.

He chose one, the biggest I could see, and climbed up onto its back. Rayna and Miyoko did the same. Then Joseph. Hood walked back to a large tree near the house, his part in our plan not needing a horse. I gave Baka a nudge and he trotted up to the front of the herd of horses. The other four followed, and soon we were lined up, five horses standing side by side, a thousand more behind us.

"Do we need to go through it again?" I asked.

"It's not that complicated," said Miyoko. "You have the hardest part."

"I know, but I'm just worried. You guys don't have the Shield to protect you."

"You think too much," said Joseph. "We ain't a bunch of pansies. Let's get it on!"

"Jimmy," Rayna said, giving Joseph a disapproving look. "We can't spend the rest of eternity hiding behind your Gifts. Forget about it. Today we fight, and we will fight to the death. Just do your part, and we'll do ours."

It wasn't that easy. Every molecule in my body was worried. "Tanaka, are you sure the *okisaru* . . ."

"YES!" he yelled. "You quit worry and we go already!"

"Okay, you're right. I just wish I could sit back and watch when they *change*." I took a deep breath and blew out a big sigh. "Then I guess we're good to go."

I nudged Baka gently with my right foot, and he stepped forward. The next thing I did, I'd been dying to do since we'd first begun formulating the attack.

I held my right arm up into the air, and called on the Ice. A quick swirl of white whipped around my hand and the air above it, forming a long flat object with sharp edges, coming to a point at the end.

A sword of Ice.

My fingers curled around its handle, and I lowered the sword until its tip pointed ahead to the pack of Shadow Ka.

"Let's ride."

CHAPTER 40
Charge

I kicked Baka into action, and he shot into a gallop, heading straight across the fields toward the sea of black. Tanaka and the others did the same, and the rest of the horses followed suit. We rode across the land in a thundering of hooves, like the chaotic beating of a thousand drums. I leaned forward, my sword of Ice pointed at our foes like a compass of death.

The Shadow Ka answered, and charged at us with the same ferocity. Some of them were flying low to the ground, but most of them were running, wings folded behind them. As we got closer, their sheer numbers almost made my heart stop. For every one of us, there seemed to be a hundred of them. And they were all big and black and brutal. Their collective screams shattered even the sound of the pounding hooves, and the world became nothing but blurs of color and deafening noise.

The two armies sped toward each other with a vengeance, ready to crash like competing tsunamis. A black horde of wings and shadows and claws and teeth coming toward a racing wave of brown muscle and five lone humans. Dust clouded up all around us as we rushed forward.

We had started several hundred feet from them. As we got closer, I was tempted more and more to start our next phase, but I knew I had to wait until the last second. We wanted them close and packed in for the next part of the plan. When they were a hundred feet away, I could see the pits where their shadowed eyes looked out, their gnashing teeth, their claws digging into the ground as they came at us.

Eighty feet. Seventy feet. Sixty feet. Their screeches and wails were unbearable.

At fifty feet, I reached my right arm behind me and threw the sword with all of my strength at the front line of the Ka. Then, with concentrated effort, I formed a long wall of Ice in the path of the Ka, stretching it out in both directions as far as I could. I thickened the wall as much as possible before the oncoming horde crashed into it, shattering the Ice. It didn't seem like much, but it was enough to slow them down.

"NOW!" I yelled.

Rayna and Miyoko split off from me and took their horses to the left. Tanaka and Joseph headed to the right, all of their horses now running parallel to the front of the oncoming Ka. The rest of the *okisaru*-horses followed my companions, half going with the ladies, the other half going with the men. I kept galloping dead ahead, so that from above I must've looked like a rocket launching from the ground with the two diverging groups of horses resembling smoke and flame shooting away from me.

I hoped we hadn't waited too long—they needed to flank the army of Ka and surround them. But I had no more time to think about it.

I slammed into the wave of angry black beasts.

The Shield formed around Baka and me in a perfect

bubble, rolling through the Ka like a massive bowling ball. Creatures blew away from me left and right, screaming and furious. They knew about my protection, but they still tried to get to me. One after another, all identical, the Shadow Ka came at me. But the Shield held.

Like debris bouncing off an armor-plated tank, they were useless against me. I drove straight through toward the heart of them, knowing what would be at their center. Every second was precious, every instant vital to our plan. If too much time went by . . .

There. Straight ahead was a glimpse of color, a break in the complete blackness—three figures, bound and surrounded by a group of Ka. I urged Baka forward, willing him to hurry. I just had to get there, reach them, and then everything would be set in motion.

The other Ka had shifted their focus and drive. Instead of racing outward, they were now surging back to the middle, confused at why I had left the others, wondering why the horses were avoiding a fight. Now all they wanted was to prevent me from getting my family.

It was exactly what we hoped they would do.

CHAPTER 41

Beast of Legend

Baka reared up when we reached the circle of Ka that guarded my family. Dad, Rusty, and Mom huddled together, dirty and frail, looking at me with a mixture of fear and hope. I knew that if I got down from Baka he would be carried away and ripped to shreds without the Shield. But that had never been part of the plan.

I formed and blasted balls of Ice at each Shadow Ka guard, blowing them forty feet away in an instant. Another wave of Ka surged forward without hesitating, but I quickly put a thirty-foot wall of Ice around my family, blocking them away from the oncoming Ka. I made the wall thicker and thicker with my thoughts. Then I put a roof on it until my family was completely surrounded.

Satisfied that it would last for a few seconds, I formed a big, hovering sphere of Ice right above the temporary structure and then made the ball rise forty feet in the air. Once it was high enough to see from hundreds of feet away, I exploded it into a million pieces.

The sign had been given.

Back at the farm, Hood saw the ball of Ice explode and didn't waste a heartbeat. He lifted the Bender Ring up over his head and dropped it. An instant later he was inside the barrier I'd created for my family. The Ka were attacking the structure with panicked intensity, ripping at the Ice with their claws and teeth. I threw all of my strength and thoughts into hurtling them away with blasts of Ice, but there were too many.

They ripped a hole in the wall and poured inside.

I kicked Baka into action and dove through after them, just to make sure that Hood had found enough time to complete his task. There was no sign of him or my family.

He'd done it.

We turned around and headed back for the farmhouse. My last part in the plan now depended on the *okisaru*.

After the army of horses had split apart from me, they'd accomplished their task and made it around the front line of the army of Ka. They then galloped away from the pack in a full run, angling away from them at forty-five degrees, trying to make the winged beasts think their whole part in the plan had been a diversion. The Ka's ability to think as one hurt them this time, and they fell for it. They abandoned chasing the *okisaru* and surged back to the middle to go after me.

Tanaka and the others had an exact method to their madness. Once they were spread far enough away from the Ka and saw that their attention was diverted, the horses on both sides angled back in both directions until the two sides met to form a circle around the black army, surrounding them. Tanaka continued to direct and command the *okisaru* until they'd created a widely spaced perimeter around the entire sea of Shadow Ka. The horses formed a perfect circle, their dotted line probably a mile or two in circumference. Then they all faced inward, waiting for the sign from me.

When the ball of Ice above my family exploded, the *okisaru* didn't need to wait for a command from Tanaka. They'd already been instructed on what to do next.

The familiar bright light flashed near the ears of the horses and then shot in a line down and back along the body of each one. The whole line of luminescence flared then, and expanded outward like a supernova, drowning the area around it with solar brilliance. A circle of light surrounded the Shadow Ka in a burst of blinding radiance.

The *okisaru* had never done something like this before. To do it they'd had to reach deep into the myths and legends of ancient history. They changed into something they'd never even dreamed of.

I was just breaking through the outer edge of the Ka, heading for the farmhouse, when I saw it. I was expecting it, and still it made my whole body tremble.

The *okisaru* had turned into dragons.

CHAPTER 42

Colored Scales

I caught my breath and spurred Baka on toward the house. To do so, we had to pass under one of the towering beasts of fantasy tales and stress-induced nightmares.

It was thirty feet tall and fifty feet long from its head to the tip of its tail. The color of its scales shifted as we passed under it, from gray to blue to purple to dark green, like an oil slick on the ocean. Four thick legs with long talons gripped the ground where it rested, supporting the main body of the beast, muscled and massive. Its head was triangular, with jagged spikes growing out of its chin like a deadly beard. The monster's yellow, slitted eyes were protected with an arch of hard, scaled skin, and another row of short spikes grew out of the top of its head and continued down the dragon's long back. The spikes ended in a double-cross of hard bone at the tip of the tail.

But the wings were the most breathtaking part. Attached to either side of the row of spikes near the shoulders in a knotted mass of skin and scales, the wings stretched out and up for another thirty feet or so, making the dragon look twice as big as it would with the wings folded in. They were veined and colorful, thick membranes of powerful muscle. They left no doubt that these creatures could fly, and fly with a vengeance.

I held my breath until we were well past the dragon, even though I knew he was on our side. At the house, I jumped off of Baka and looked back. The sight of a thousand dragons stretching out and around the Shadow Ka was an image that I knew would be sealed forever in my mind. I stared, transfixed by what I saw, and found it hard to believe.

Miyoko and the others rode on the backs of the giant winged lizards, directing them, urging them on. Somewhere in the distance I heard the faintest trace of Tanaka yelling out a command.

The dragons took to the air and attacked the Shadow Ka.

CHAPTER 43

Body

The whole purpose of our plan from the beginning had been twofold.

First, we had to get my family without taking any risks of the Ka deciding it wasn't worth it to keep them alive. After that, we had to make sure that none of the Ka escaped, not one. What better way to accomplish that than a thousand fire-breathing dragons that were ten times bigger than a Shadow Ka? And that had also been the reason for setting up the complete circle surrounding our enemy.

I watched as the dragons split into two groups—one staying back to protect the perimeter, the other moving in for the kill. I'd made it clear that we were supposed to keep as many alive as possible. But by the same token, we couldn't allow any resistance or escape. If it came down to the lives of humans or the lives of Shadow Ka, there was no hard decision to be made. And so I knew that in the end, many of the Ka would die in those fields. And despite their evil, it made me sad because deep down they still had to have some sense of humanity left in them.

The attacking group of dragons had reached the outer edge of the Ka, and landed on the ground, facing forward and ready to fight. Although I couldn't see Tanaka, I knew he was out there, somehow giving commands. Right now he was telling them to wait—to let the Ka be the first to attack.

And attack they did.

From somewhere deep in the black, writhing mass of Ka, a cry rung out—the terrible, haunting sound of someone dying in agony. But I knew it was a Ka, and I knew it was an order. As one, thousands of Ka sprang forward and attacked the standing ring of dragons. With outstretched claws and teeth the black creatures rushed forward, oblivious to the consequences. They had to know it was suicide, but they went forward anyway with all of their strength, tearing and ripping anything that came in their path.

It was then that the dragons started breathing out the fire.

Great, spouting flames exploded out of their huge mouths, incinerating anything and everything that got in the way. The charging screams of the Ka turned into wrenching cries of fear. Shadow Ka were running in all directions, alight with fire, falling and tripping over each other and then lying still. Hundreds must have died in a matter of minutes. The rest quickly gave up and surged back together in a tight pack, now noticeably smaller than when the fight had started. But they still outnumbered the *okisaru*.

The Ka now had no doubt about their chances of surviving this fight. And so they chose the only alternative. They flew up into the sky, desperate to escape.

They had barely reached thirty feet before the outside ring of dragons shot into the air, chasing and herding the Ka, cutting off all routes of escape. Some got through, like flies through a hole in a window screen. But the dragons stopped the stragglers with bursting spouts of flame, enveloping them with liquid heat before they could get very far.

Fear was the key. Eventually, the Ka would give in to the fear, and surrender. No matter how noble they thought their cause, in the end they would choose life over death. Especially death by incineration. So many already lay on the ground, writhing in agony.

I couldn't watch anymore. Victory seemed pretty certain, and I wanted to see my family. I turned and ran into the house.

"Mom! Dad!" I yelled as I ran through the front hallway and through the kitchen. "Rusty! Where are you guys?"

"In here," a voice said from the living room. It was Rusty.

I went in there, ready to throw everything aside for a moment and have a family reunion. But I stopped dead in my tracks in the entryway, stunned by what I saw.

Hood was sitting on the couch, his head resting against his Ring. His arms and legs were bound with a tough cord. Rusty sat on one side of him, Dad on the other, also bound. Even as I began to take in what else was in the room, I froze the cords with Ice and shattered them apart. But they didn't move.

That's because my mom was being held by a big Shadow Ka, one of its black arms wrapped around her neck. They stood by the fireplace, and at their feet lay a body, already showing the ghostly white skin of death.

I knew she wasn't just asleep, caught in the Black Coma. Inori was dead.

CHAPTER 44

Knifepoint

The Ka morphed into a human, its reverse evolution now so normal that it didn't even faze me. And I wasn't the least bit surprised when I saw who it was.

Raspy.

He still held my mom around the neck, and in his other hand was a knife.

"Make one move and she'll join your lady friend here," he said, his voice full of its usual phlegm. "I know what you're thinking. Can you freeze my hand before I do the damage? Care to test it?"

I stared at him, furious, but not yet knowing what to do. I waited.

"You think you've won?" he continued. "Do you really think that defeating my brothers, the Ka, is all it will take?" He spat on the ground. "You will never, never beat the Stompers. Never."

"Well, we'll just have to find out, won't we?"

"Oh, you'll find out, sure enough. I wish I could be there when you see what they have in store for you. You soon will understand fear, my boy."

"Would you please shut up?" I said. "Now let go of my mom."

"Let go? Just like that? I don't think so. I want my freedom."

"Freedom? You think I'm going to let you walk out of here after all you've done to me?"

"Yes, I do. If you want your mother to live any longer."

I shook my head and laughed. "Raspy, it amazes me how often you underestimate my Gifts."

With a scant thought, I slammed his legs and arms back against the mantle of the fireplace, pinned there with solid beams of Ice. The knife dropped from his hand and clanked against the bricks. He struggled to free himself, but it was useless.

Mom burst into tears and ran over to me, clasping me in a big hug. Dad and Rusty joined in a second later. I continued to stare at Raspy.

"Good plan, Tiger," I said to him. "That worked really well. Have fun hanging up there for a while."

Black veins suddenly shot through his skin and he began the transition back into a Shadow Ka. I put more thoughts into the Ice, strengthening its hold on his limbs. The power of it was too great, and Raspy gave up and turned back into a human. Otherwise, the Ice probably would've cut his arms and legs off as they grew into the much bigger limbs of a Ka.

"Stop it, Raspy," I said. "Just stop it. It's over. You're beat."

And then I relaxed, closed my eyes, and allowed myself a few seconds to enjoy the hug from my family.

When they let go, I went over to Inori. I knelt beside her and touched her forehead. It was ice-cold. Her chest was not moving, and when I put my fingers on her neck just like they do in the movies, there was no pulse.

"What happened?" I asked in a sullen voice.

"She was dead when we got here," Dad said. "Hood showed up with his Ring right after you made that Ice wall around us. He took Mom and Rusty on the first trip and then came back for me just seconds later. When we popped up in here, I saw Inori lying right there and Custer had already grabbed your mom."

"When we came," Rusty said, "he was hunched over her, but I couldn't tell what he was doing. Then he grabbed Mom and held her with his two wings while he tied us up, threatening her the whole time. You sicko!" Rusty picked up a small porcelain figurine from an end table and threw it at Raspy. It shattered against his chest.

He tried to hide it, but I could tell that it hurt him.

"Do whatever makes you feel better, boy," he said. "It won't change things when your brother goes to meet my masters."

I formed a gag of Ice and stuffed it in his mouth. He mumbled and gurgled and thrashed about as much as he could.

"I told you to be quiet."

I looked back down at Inori, at her pale, dead face, and my heart felt crushed. I hadn't known her that well, but her desire to help us and to win this war had touched me greatly. But I couldn't find any tears for her—maybe I'd used them all up by then.

I stood up. "Raspy, you will pay for this, and for all your other crimes. Especially for killing my grandpa. Rusty, if you feel like throwing anything else at him, go ahead."

He bent over to pick up another trinket.

"No," said Mom. "That's enough."

That's when I noticed the crumpled piece of paper, clasped in Inori's dead hand.

CHAPTER 45

Note from the Dead

It took quite an effort to wiggle the paper out of her cold hand. She must've used all her strength to protect it in her last moments.

I finally freed the note and we ran into the kitchen to get away from Raspy. I spread it out on the table, smoothing out the wrinkles.

It was addressed to me.

Dear Jimmy,

I've sent Half away, because I fear what may happen. I could not risk losing him to the Shadow Ka. That is also why I write you this note. Just in case.

I quit reading. "Holy crud, I forgot about Half. Has anyone seen him?"

All I got were negative head shakes. I turned back to the note.

You must find Half. He is the only one who can help you find the Dream Warden. Then you must capture a

Shadow Ka and force him to take you and the Warden of Dreams to the Yumeka, to the Stompers.

You cannot do this without the Warden. And the Grand Exception.

It will not be as you may think. The Gifts will help, but in the end, only one thing will save you. You must conquer your fear.

I wish victory upon you.

Inori

I shrank back into a sitting position on the floor.

"Boy, she really cleared things up, didn't she?" Rusty said.

"You're not kidding," I said. "Come on, we have to find Half, and then deal with the Shadow Ka."

"Did someone say my name? And who the heck is that guy?"

I turned in shock, although I shouldn't have been surprised. Half was in the doorway, staring at Raspy in the other room.

"Where did you go?" I asked.

"Inori made me . . ." His words stopped when he saw her on the ground. "Oh my . . ." We followed as he ran to her and grabbed her hand. "What—"

I explained everything to him, and his face went white.

"I should've been here," he said, devastated. "I could've saved her. Especially considering I could've left one of me here to watch from the corner, just to make sure she was okay."

I still had a hard time when he talked about how he could split up and be in different places. I grabbed him and made everyone go back into the kitchen.

"Half, then maybe you'd be dead too." I said as we walked. "She said in this note that I needed you to find the Dream Warden."

"She . . . she made me leave. I didn't get it—she made me stay, and then as soon as you were gone she made me go away. I kept telling her I should stay here, but she got all mad and screamed at me. Then I left because she'd ticked me off."

He sat down at the table, put his head in his hands, and went silent.

"Half, this isn't your fault," said Dad. "Inori knew what she was doing."

He looked up, his eyes red. "I don't know anything about the stupid Dream Warden. I don't know what she's talking about!"

"You've gotta know something," I said. "She wrote that you were the only one who could find him."

"I'm telling you, I don't know anything!"

The room went silent, and I sat and stared at him for a moment, thinking through things. It just wasn't adding up.

"Come on," I finally said. "Let's go take care of the Ka, and then we can worry about it."

Reluctant to leave Inori alone, but not knowing what else to do, we walked outside.

Everything was in perfect order.

The tight pack of Shadow Ka showed no movement, an almost endless sea of silent, subdued black creatures. The dragons stood at their posts, surrounding them, ready to squash any more ideas of escape.

We had won the battle. The Shadow Ka were defeated.

Almost.

There was one more thing to do.

CHAPTER 46

Travel Plans

Tanaka, Joseph, Rayna, and Miyoko came walking up from the battlefield—dirty, bleeding, and exhausted by the looks of it. But they bore the faces of victors, and Tanaka was even smiling.

"We did it, Jimmy-san!" he yelled. "You tell the world they not mess with General Tanaka, *neh?*"

"Yeah, those dragons didn't help you at all, did they?"

"No, they help a little." He laughed, and gave his daughter a big hug. "Miyoko here actually punched Ka in face—I saw it happen!"

Miyoko raised her arm and showed her biceps. "No problem."

"Wow, guys," I said, "we actually pulled it off. Tanaka, can you tell the *okisaru* how thankful I am?"

"Yes, I can. Once the Ka are gone."

"Oh, yeah, that little part."

"What're you going to do?" asked Dad.

"Well, I learned a little trick back in Japan under Mount

Fuji." I turned and looked at my dad. "Just sit back and enjoy the show."

I walked forward until I was thirty or forty feet away from the nearest Ka. Most of them stood, wings drooping, heads sagging. It was so bizarre to see them this way, humbled and defeated. I couldn't help but wonder what went on inside their heads—if the human side and the Ka side battled with each other. Maybe when I went to college I would write a thesis on the subject. For now, I had more important things to worry about.

I held my hands out, and tried to take the whole group of Ka into my vision. Then I called upon the Ice, and formed it in and around every Ka, growing it and pushing it out more and more. I froze the legs and wings of the countless hordes of Ka, then I froze them into bigger chunks of Ice, and then I froze those pieces together. More and more, thicker and thicker, spreading out until it covered the whole army of creatures, and covered every inch of the fields they stood on.

My muscles strained with the effort, but I kept going. The usual swirls and tornadoes of white mist flew in and around the Ka as the Ice formed, freezing them together in one massive structure but leaving their heads free to breathe.

I finished, and bent over in exhaustion.

"Tanaka, tell the *okisaru* to make sure I got all of them," I said through deep breaths.

He yelled out something to a nearby dragon, and it lifted into the air. It flew in an arc above the Shadow Ka, and then made a pass over the entire group. It came back a minute later and settled to the ground in a cloud of dust.

I wasn't sure how it communicated with Tanaka, but he turned to me and said, "There are none who are free."

I walked back to my family, turned, and got a better look.

For as far as we could see, a four-foot layer of Ice covered the fields, with the bottom half of every last Shadow Ka frozen into it, like some deranged dessert for giants. Shadow Ka Delight perhaps.

They wiggled and groaned with the effort to escape, but they had no hope. They were all caught in the Ice.

"I'll be back," I said.

I went inside and released Raspy but then quickly formed a leash of thick Ice around his neck.

"Come on," I told him. "If you try to escape I'll send a dragon after you."

Surprisingly, he said nothing and followed me outside without resistance, my hand clasping the long Ice rope attached to his neck.

Once outside and facing the iceberg full of struggling Ka, I released his frozen leash into the air and then grabbed him around the neck with my own hand.

"I know you can talk to each other in your minds. Tell them, Raspy—tell them that they have one last chance to come back in their hearts, to come back to the good. If they do, the waters of the Blackness won't kill them, just like it spared my dad. But if not, it'll burn away their evil until there's nothing left. Tell them."

"I'll say no such thing to my loyal brothers."

I let go of him and shook my head.

"Then let it be on your shoulders."

I turned to the fields. The massive structure of Ice and Shadow loomed before us, filling our entire vision. But I knew how the Second Gift worked now, and I felt I could do this.

Closing my eyes, I called upon the Ice again but in a

different way. I fed it with my thoughts, told it exactly what I wanted to happen. I let my Gift do all the work. Images burned and flickered across my mind, and then all went black. I opened my eyes.

The captured Shadow Ka were heading for the sky. Like a mega mother spaceship departing from its last conquered world, the huge plane of ice and beasts floated upward. It soon hovered over us, defying every law of gravity in the book. From the bottom it looked filthy—full of dirt and grime and grass. Not to mention the countless clawed feet that were just visible through the thin layer of ice between them and us.

Up it went, higher and higher, the Ka's screams fading across the distance. Once it had gained sufficient altitude, the structure flew north, picking up speed slowly but surely. We all watched in fascination as it grew smaller and smaller, and finally was a black dot against the gray skies. I'd sent them to the one place in the world I knew for sure was still ripped open to the Blackness.

I'd sent them on their way home, never to come back.

CHAPTER 47

The Half

We went into the house to rest and eat. I secured Raspy to the same place in the living room—chained with Ice to the bricks of the fireplace. He was beginning to look sicker and more pale than usual, and I worried that he would die on me.

"Raspy, what's wrong with you?" I asked him. "Being a human getting you down?"

"You don't get it, do you?" he said.

"Get what?"

"How it all works. What we are, how we became Ka, what *really* is going on."

"I have no idea what you're talking about, but I'm not going to let you poison me with your lies."

He started to say something more but I gagged him again with a chunk of Ice.

"It was nice talking to you," I said. "Really, I mean it." I began to walk back to the kitchen and then stopped. "Don't worry, we'll bring you some food—I'm not that cruel."

He tried to mumble through the ice but I ignored him.

Dad cooked up a nice meal of grits and eggs and sausage—thankfully my uncle had a huge freezer in the basement that was well stocked. He must've been a good scout as a child and learned to be prepared. As we dug in and devoured every bite, I couldn't remember a time when food had tasted so good.

There we sat, mostly in silence, around the big table. My family, Joseph, the members of the Alliance. Half looked especially troubled.

"Twice, what's wrong?" He didn't catch my joke about his name, so I threw a small piece of sausage at him.

He snapped out of his daze. "What?"

"What's wrong?" I repeated.

"Nothing—I just feel so awful about Inori. I mean, she's lying in that room as we speak!"

"It isn't your fault," said Dad. "And we'll make certain to go out and give her a proper burial."

"Joseph," I asked. "Do you think it would be too late to send her into the Blackness to try to save her?" There was a healing power about that place—it had saved Joseph's life and healed my dad's gunshot wound.

"I'm sorry, little buddy, but I think it's too late. Remember, I wasn't dead yet when Dontae dumped me through the Black Curtain. Close but not dead. There's nothing we can do for your friend."

"I just hate it that we battled all those Ka out there while one of them was in here killing one of our own. It's just stupid!"

No one answered back, and the thought hung in the air.

"Plus, I needed her for the next part," I continued. "Her

note didn't help us at all—at least that's what you said, Half. Are you sure . . ."

"I'm telling you, I've never heard of a stinking Dream Warden. And I've been around, I promise."

Another few minutes passed in silence, and then I went into the other room to grab my leather case. It lay right next to Inori—she must have held onto it until the very end. Raspy looked at me as I walked about, but I ignored him.

I carried the pack into the other room, and pulled out the Red Disk that wasn't red anymore. I held it in front of me, amazed once again at how it reflected everything but my face.

"Let me see that stupid thing," said Half.

I handed it to him, and he tilted it side to side slightly, just like I had done. I waited for his comment on how weird it was to see a mirror that didn't work quite right.

A smile broke across his face—his usual smug expression that we hadn't seen in a while.

"Dang," he said, "I am one good looking son of a gun."

My heart stopped for three full seconds.

CHAPTER 48

Warden of Dreams

"What do you mean?" I asked, standing up so fast that my chair fell backward.

"Huh?" he looked surprised at my reaction. "You got a problem with my looks or what?"

"What . . ." Then I realized he hadn't heard the story about the Disk. He had no idea what was going on.

"Half, can you see yourself in that mirror?" I asked.

"Can I see myself . . . what's wrong with you, man?"

"Can you?"

"Can I . . . of course I can."

I walked around the table until I was behind him. Then I reached forward to steady the Disk in front of his face again. He looked back at me in the mirror.

"Oh my gosh, I can't believe it."

The others were looking at me like I was nuts, and I realized that *none* of them had heard the story. Everything had been crazy from the instant Hood brought Inori and me back from New York.

"You guys, he can see himself. Do you know what that means?"

I was met with blank stares. I grabbed the Disk out of his hands and walked around the room, shoving it in everyone's face. One by one, they saw the absence of their reflection, and surprise and confusion filled the room like helium in a balloon.

"Only one person in the world shows up in this mirror," I said. I walked back to Half, made him stand up and put his back to the others. I put the Disk in front of his face and tilted it so that the others could see his reflection. I dropped the mirror to my side, stared at him for a second, and then turned to the others.

"The Half is the Dream Warden."

I had to take a few minutes and catch everyone up on what had happened with Inori and Farmer. I told them about the Riddle of the Red Disk—that you needed the Disk, in other words, a mirror, to realize the truth behind Erifani Tup, and you needed the truth behind Erifani Tup, or Put In A Fire, to figure out that the Red Disk was a mirror.

That part was hard to explain, but I told them the point was that whoever showed up in the mirror was the Dream Warden, and was supposed to help me beat the Stompers by using the Grand Exception for everyone on the planet. I told them about Farmer, and the Fourth Gift, and anything else I could think of.

"Now we just have to figure out how to do it," I said, mentally exhausted from trying to explain everything. "Half, how can you be the Dream Warden and not know about it?"

"I'm telling you, man, I don't know anything about it. So how in the world would I know *why* I don't know anything about it? Just because I can have more than one brain at the same time doesn't mean I'm that much smarter than everyone else."

I gave him a blank look. "Good point. I guess."

"Well," said Joseph, "maybe we should sleep on it. Let the old juices stew a while as we sleep. We'll figure it out."

"Yeah," said Mom, "and I guess we don't have to worry about the Ka coming after us."

We talked a little while longer, mostly about nothing, and then went our separate ways to try and get some rest. As I lay there, looking up at the ceiling, I thought about how weird it was that I was getting some sleep so that tomorrow I could go back to sleep to meet the Stompers. But I told myself that nothing should seem weird anymore, and five minutes later I was dead to the world.

It was still dark, hours later, when Half shook me awake, his face frantic.

"What's going on?" I asked.

"I've figured it out," he said. "I know what it means to be the Dream Warden."

CHAPTER 49

What It Means

I told him to hold off until I got everyone else awake so that we'd have all of our minds together to hear his theory. He was anxious to get it out, but I made him wait.

Dawn was only a few minutes away by the time we got all the groggy, straggling people back into the kitchen and around the table. Dawn had taken on a new meaning as the gray taint of the Shadow Ka had grown worse and worse—the sunrise was more of a lessening of darkness than an increase of light anymore. But with the Ka gone now, I wondered how long it would be before the taint left the world.

Mom got some juice and toast going, and then I told Half to tell us what all the fuss was about.

"Okay, I could barely sleep trying to think through this," he began. "But, I figured that Disk thing can't tell a lie, so I'm the Dream Warden whether I want to be or not. Therefore, I decided it was up to me to figure things out."

"Half, I'm proud of you," said Rayna.

"What are you, his mother?" I asked, trying to be funny.

She looked at me and nodded, and I almost choked on a sip of orange juice.

"What?" I yelled.

"I'm just kidding," she said, with the faintest trace of a smile.

I couldn't believe it. Rayna had told a joke.

"Excuse me," said Half. "May I continue please?"

"Sorry. Do it," I replied, feeling dumb for being so gullible.

"Anyway, from what I understand about all of this—from what Farmer and Inori told Jimmy, and the bits and pieces I've learned throughout the years—I think I understand now."

He narrowed his eyes in concentration, and leaned forward.

"I don't think the Dream Warden has any power whatsoever. I think that's where we've been wrong from the beginning. That's not his role—which is why the Fourth Gift given to Jimmy is the power to control the Yumeka, whatever that means."

"So what is his role? Your role?" asked Miyoko.

"Well, it can't just be a coincidence that I'm the Warden. I mean, my ability to split myself into two or three or whatever—there has to be a reason I have that."

He paused for a minute. "Sorry, I just want to make sure I've thought through everything. Okay, so I have this weird gift, and I'm the Dream Warden. They have to be connected, and I'm pretty sure I know why." He paused again.

"Why?" Dad asked. "You're killing us here!"

"It all has to do with the Grand Exception."

"What do you mean?" I asked.

He looked straight into my eyes.

"I think I'm supposed to trigger the Exception for

everybody on the earth. Sacrifice myself and replace them. All of them."

The meaning of his words was so vast, the implications so high, that his brief statement didn't do it justice. We all sat there, dead silent, trying to sort it out.

"I don't get it," said Rusty.

"The Grand Exception," I said, understanding it fully now. "Any person can willingly replace someone trapped in the Yumeka by the Stompers. And they can't do anything about it. It's some kind of law of the universe or something." I looked at Half. "And he's saying that he can split himself into billions of people and replace all of them."

"What?" asked Joseph. "That's about the craziest thing I've ever heard."

Rayna looked sick with worry. "Half, you've never split into more than four or five places. How on earth do you think you could handle something on that scale?'

"I don't know," he said. "I don't think it's exactly the same thing as what I've done in the past—it's a combination of that with whatever it means to be the Dream Warden. I feel like I didn't become the Warden until Jimmy figured out the Red Disk. I think it's been my purpose in life from the beginning, and what I've done up to now was just a taste of the gift, a preparation for when this day would come. I know this is right, I can feel it."

"But wait a minute," said Tanaka. "I thought Jimmy-san was supposed to save the world."

"He is," replied Half.

"How he do it if you the one caught in the world of the Stompers?"

"I'm just the first step, the one who paves the way for Jimmy.

Once I'm in there, and once everyone else has been taken out of it, only one thing more has to happen."

"What's that?" asked Miyoko.

Half stood up, walked over to me, and patted my shoulder.

"Jimmy uses the Grand Exception to replace me. He'll be the only one there."

I swallowed, and knew he was right.

"Then," said Joseph, "the real battle will begin."

CHAPTER 50

Raspy

And so it was settled. Half would execute the Grand Exception, using his bizarre gift to split himself and set off a chain reaction that would result in him being the only and last one from our world captured by the Stompers. And then I would execute my one chance at the Exception, and take his place. It was exciting and scary all at once.

Now there was only one problem: convincing Raspy to do the dirty work to get us there.

It ended up being far easier than we could've imagined. That's because we just happened to forget to tell him that little part about Half and his unusual abilities.

"You want me to put you in the Coma?" Raspy asked when we approached him an hour or so after Half told us everything. "The Grand Exception? You really are as stupid as I thought." I knew we couldn't play too dumb, or Raspy would see there was something more going on, so I told him the truth about my part.

"You've known from the beginning that in the end I

would have to meet the Stompers, Raspy. I plan on winning that battle. And you're going to send me there."

He laughed, spit flying out of his mouth.

"I've told you before boy, there is no way you can win. If I send you there, you will only be doing exactly what they want you to do. Their victory will be complete with you trapped in the Yumeka forever."

"I'm willing to take that chance."

"You're an idiot, boy!" he yelled, taking me aback. "Who cares about the rest of them! You can run away, go into the Blackness and find another world. Leave these . . . humans to their fate."

"I can't do that."

"Why? You think yourself so noble? We'll see how that nobility serves you when you beg the Stompers for mercy."

"Well, good. Then you'll win. So will you do it or not?"

He grinned, and let out a long, wheezy cackle.

"On one condition."

"And what's that?" I asked.

"You let me send all of you. Everyone, no exceptions."

It was exactly what we hoped he would say.

"But that just means other people somewhere else will be released," I said, "since we'll all be doing it voluntarily, invoking the Exception."

"Pah! I don't care, as long as you and your group here live in misery the rest of your lives."

I had to put up a fight, or he would see through our plan.

"Raspy, I could end it right now, send you back to the

Blackness and have you thrown in the waters. You know that would kill you."

"Go ahead. Then you'll have failed in saving your world. Either way, I win, and you lose."

"Raspy!" I yelled.

"Take it or leave it, as you would say."

I glared at him, trying my best to throw all the hatred I could into my eyes. Although I was acting when it came to disagreeing with his proposal, the hatred part was easy. And he bought it.

"Fine," I said. "Send all of us. That's just more people to help me win."

I turned to walk out of the room. "Get yourself ready," I said over my shoulder. "We're doing it in thirty minutes."

There wasn't much to do in the way of preparation for us. We were as rested as we could be, and filled up with food. Not a one of us had the slightest clue of what to expect once we entered the Black Coma. We still weren't entirely sure what that meant. The Yumeka was still something that baffled us.

And yet, we were going into the heart of it. It amazed me that after all this time of fighting the Shadow Ka and avoiding their dark purpose, I was about to lie down and willingly allow Raspy to take me to his masters. It also scared me to death.

The Stompers. The first time I ever heard that word was when my dad took me to the airport to send me to Utah. Ever since that day I'd been told how terrible they were but never really anything specific. What did it mean to be a nightmare? Their own name, Stompers, didn't make sense until recently.

After all this, after all the blood and heartache and terror, I was finally going to face them.

It was a new kind of fear for me. It was the fear of the unknown.

And this time, the fear was being brought to me at my own request.

We spoke together in the kitchen, trying to plan out events as best we could. The trust we placed in Half's theory was enormous, and everything depended on it. But it made sense—it made complete sense.

When it was time, we filed into the living room. I released Raspy from his bindings, ready to retaliate if he did something crazy. He could tell I was watching him closely.

"Boy, you have nothing to worry about. What you've asked of me—it's exactly what I want to do. I just can't believe you have the stupidity to go willingly."

"You just send us, Raspy. If they win, I'll buy you dinner."

"Jimmy," said Joseph, "how do you know he won't kill us once we're all asleep?"

"He can't kill me," I said. "I have the Shield, remember?"

"Well, what about us?" asked Rusty.

"I don't think he'd dare."

Raspy snorted in disgust. "You people are making me ill. Don't you know the rules? The Stompers forbid the termination of any person unless it's by them. It is a law that we would never break, not even for scum like you."

"Why would they have such a rule?" Mom asked.

"Because they want the power of termination for themselves," answered Raspy.

"What about the members of the Alliance that were killed?" I asked.

"It was done in their dreams by my masters."

"What about Rayna and Joseph—your friends sure tried to get rid of them."

"No, we sent them into the Blackness to be healed. Always, we try. If we fail, we pay the price."

"Then why did you kill Inori, you animal!" yelled Half.

"I didn't!" Raspy roared, spit flying from his mouth. "You all assumed it but never asked, did you?"

"What?" I said, incredulous. "You didn't kill her?"

"No." He said it quietly, and looked down.

"I don't believe him," said Rusty.

"You don't believe me?" Raspy said, looking up in anger. "You think I'm foolish enough to disobey the Stompers?"

"Then how did she die?" I asked.

Raspy grew quiet, and looked away. Something bothered him about all of this.

"Tell us, Raspy," I said with a stern voice.

"She . . . died of a broken heart."

"A broken heart?" said Rusty. "That's about the dumbest thing I've heard from your nasty old mouth, and that's saying something."

Raspy keyed his eyes in on Rusty, their blackness boiling with hatred. But then it faded, and he looked down again.

"Raspy," I said. "Tell us!"

He looked at me, and for the first time since I'd met him, he looked human.

"She was my daughter. I will say no more."

CHAPTER 51

The Black Coma

His revelation stunned us into complete silence.

"How . . ." I began, but he cut me off.

"I told you I will say no more. I said 'was' and I meant it. She means nothing to me now."

"Means nothing?" my mom asked, unable to comprehend such a thing. "How could your own daughter mean nothing?"

"What about my grandpa?" I asked.

"I killed him before I was fully complete. And I paid dearly for it."

"What . . ."

"Enough!" he screamed. "One more word about it, and I will leave. The discussion is over."

"Fine," I said. "I pick the order, and I want to be last. You'll do my family first, then Rayna, Tanaka, Hood, and Miyoko. Then Joseph. Then Half. Then me."

"What does it matter?" he asked, his suspicion rising just a little.

"It doesn't. But that's how I want it done, and it's not up for negotiation."

Raspy chuckled. "You think you have a plan, don't you? Do you really think it matters? You want yourself and the others to pull your family back out using the Exception, right? That's not the deal. I want them there to suffer with you."

I hadn't hoped for something this good. He had caught on enough to think something was fishy but not so much that it would ruin our real plan.

"Does it matter?" I asked. "They'll have me—that's all that you should care about."

"No," he said. "I told you I would only do this if you all go. I don't care if you replace other people, but I want everyone in this room there, with the Stompers."

"Fine. Just do it." It didn't matter anyway.

"I am happy to oblige."

A shudder went through the air as he morphed into the massive shape of the Shadow Ka. He whipped his black wings in the air, and let out a short cry. It was even worse indoors. It ripped through my ears and pummeled my nerves. Everyone around me shook in fear as the reality of what we had agreed to settled in.

Raspy walked over to my dad, pointed his black, beastly muzzle at him, staring with those empty eyes. Then he spoke.

It was the first time I'd ever been able to understand words coming from a Ka. It was whispery and metallic, and sent goose bumps popping up all over my skin.

"Do you invoke the Grand Exception?" he asked, the words slithering through the air like possessed radio waves.

"Uh . . . yes . . . yes I do," Dad said.

"Who do you sacrifice for?"

Dad was silent for a second, and then spoke the name.

"Darin Fincher."

Raspy screamed his song of darkness into the air. We clamped our hands to our ears, reeling from the pain. It was terrible and loud. I knew that somewhere in the world, my uncle was waking up, surprised for sure.

Dad crumpled to the floor.

CHAPTER 52

The Grand Exception

Mom was next.

Raspy stared her down, breathing loudly.

"Do you invoke the Grand Exception?"

"Yes," she said with a trembling voice. It broke my heart to see her so afraid, and I hated myself for doing this to her.

"Whom do you sacrifice for?"

"My husband, you sick son of a biscuit eater."

Despite the circumstances, I groaned out loud in sarcasm. "You tell him, Mom."

"My husband. J. M. Fincher."

As Raspy screamed again, Dad woke up, dazed and shaking, just as Mom fell to the floor.

Raspy morphed back into his human form.

"This was not the deal!" he screamed. "You promised me they would all go into the Coma with you!"

I was fed up.

"You know what, *Custer?* Just forget the Exception, anyway. Take them. Take them all without replacing anyone. I give you permission, and I won't interfere."

"What about you?"

"I think the Shield will protect me somehow, but then I plan on invoking the Exception to get in anyway. And I promise I won't replace anyone in my family. Fair enough?" My promise was actually a very true one.

"How can I trust you?"

"Does it matter? Criminy, man, all that matters is that you get me there so the Stompers can destroy me, right? Just do it!"

In a quick flash of black, he turned into a Ka. He started singing again, although this time it was a little different. But it was still a grating, shrieking sound that hurt my ears. What he didn't notice is that I moved closer to Half and touched his hand with my finger, extending the Shield to protect him as well.

When we were on the boat out on the ocean, and the Ka had started hypnotizing everyone into the Coma, it hadn't worked on me. I had grown sleepy, but everyone else dropped to the floor way before I got even close. It had to have been the Shield, and I counted on it now.

Mom was already gone, but everyone else's eyes got droopy, and then their bodies began to sway back and forth. A few seconds later, they all collapsed to the ground as one.

All except for Half. And me.

Raspy looked at us with his black eyes. His head tilted to the side in confusion.

"Sorry, I accidentally touched Half and protected him, too," I said. It sounded so dumb when it came out I grimaced without meaning to.

"It's okay," Half said before Raspy could begin to think. "I want to invoke the Exception—and not for Jimmy's family."

Raspy said and did nothing.

"For my friend . . . for John Richards," Half blurted out. The name sounded made up, and reminded me of a short fat kid I knew growing up. But it convinced Raspy.

He stepped closer to Half until his black muzzle almost touched the Dream Warden's nose.

"Do you wish to invoke the Grand Exception?" he breathed out with his metallic voice. The formality of the whole thing seemed so bizarre.

"Yes."

"Whom do you sacrifice for?"

"Well," said Half, smiling. "I changed my mind."

"What do you mean?" whispered Raspy.

"I choose everyone. Everyone on our entire planet."

The Shadow Ka laughed, a wet and gurgling sound that made my skin crawl. But then he began to sing his song, and Half fell to the floor. Raspy morphed into a human.

"Is your friend really so delusional?" he asked me. "I don't know what he thought he was . . ."

He stopped in midsentence. The others in the room—my dad, Rusty, everyone—were waking up, rubbing their eyes, looking around in a dazed shock.

It had worked.

My mom's face was pale and taut, like she'd just been through a crash course on how to be a serial killer. I hurt inside again, imagining what she must have gone through, even for those brief moments.

"What is this?" asked Raspy, more confused than angry. "How did you come back?"

"Forget it," I said to him. "You have one more to do."

"How . . . how is this happening?" he asked again. "What have you done!"

"We've released them, Raspy. All of them. Now help me—I want to invoke the Exception."

"No!" he screamed, his eyes darting about. "No! It's over, I'm done! What have you done to me? What is happening?" He grew delirious, thrashing about at nothing with his old, frail arms. "How have you tricked me?" he yelled.

"You don't need to know. Now invoke the Exception!"

"No! I won't!"

"Yes, you will!" I screamed, stepping up to him. I grabbed his shirt.

"You don't have a choice. I choose it, and it's a law. Now do it!"

"No!"

"Then I'll do it for you, Raspy. I choose to invoke the Grand Exception."

"NO!" he said again.

"I choose to sacrifice," I said with a stern voice. "I choose Justin, the Half. I sacrifice for him, for the Dream Warden. Now do it."

Against his own wishes, Raspy turned back into a Shadow Ka.

Then he began to sing his song.

CHAPTER 53

Into the Yumeka

I released the Shield from its protective power.

A wave of invisible force hit me, like silent thunder. My vision changed, and Raspy looked distorted, as if he were on the other side of a veil of water. I felt tired, more so than ever before in my life. Sleep beckoned, reached for me, grabbed me. The Black Coma called me to it, to the Yumeka, to the realm of the Stompers.

Before I let myself go, I turned my head to the others. It was hard to do—already everything felt like the dream where you can't make yourself move, even though a train is coming at you. I forced out some last words, although I couldn't tell if they heard me.

"I don't know if I'll make it back. But I promise I won't fail."

I closed my eyes.

CHAPTER 54

Into the Stompers

My eyes snap open, and I realize that I'm dreaming.

I'm in a parking lot, late at night, no cars. The air smells of asphalt and gasoline. The lights of downtown Atlanta sparkle like Christmas lights around me. It's cold, and there's a wind blowing. I know this is nothing but a dream, and I wonder if this is the Yumeka.

Then something breathes next to me, and I jump in surprise.

It's a dark shape, and as my eyes settle in on its enormity, I realize it's a Shadow Ka. Something tells me it's not Raspy—that it's not even a real one.

"This is a dream," I say. "I don't get it. Is this the Yumeka?"

"No," the Ka says with the same unusual voice as Raspy. "The difference is hard to understand."

He screams a shrieking cry like the one heard back in my uncle's house. The silent thunder passes over me again, and the air around me seems to bend.

It snaps back like a whip and . . .

I wasn't dreaming anymore. I still stood in the same

parking lot, looking at the Ka, cold in the dark of night. But the same feeling washed over me that I had when I first met Inori. It felt real—nothing like the hazy, vague feeling of a dream.

It was the Yumeka. The place where dreams and reality met in a world that was more than each one could be by itself. The place where the Stompers thrived and conquered.

"I don't know what you've done," the Shadow Ka said. "But it's in the hands of my masters now."

He reached his huge, clawed hands forward and grabbed my shirt. He pulled me close to him then wrapped both arms around me in a tight grip. His wings snapped in the air and we took flight. I knew this was part of it from the stories I'd heard from Joseph and Rayna. I knew where we were going.

The parking lot shrunk as we quickly gained altitude, passing up and over the tall buildings of Atlanta. My stomach jumped into my throat as the Ka banked hard and flew toward the east. His wings thumped with each flap, and a strong wind blew against us as he gained speed.

"Why does the Yumeka look just like my own world?" I yelled to the Ka.

"Because it is one and the same," he said back. No one ever seemed to give me an answer that made the least bit of sense.

The sun broke through the plane of the horizon, a sharp ray of light piercing my vision. The sky was cloudless, but instead of the purples and blues of early morning, it was gray and black, like watching an old TV show. I looked below and was shocked to see that we were over the ocean, its waters dark and ominous. *How had we gotten this far?* I wondered.

It was then that I first saw the big face of myself, looking back at me.

This too I had expected.

It appeared out of nowhere—not there one second, there the next. It was massive, as large as any building I'd ever seen, and floated in the air above the ocean. The structure was a perfect replica of my face, carved out of the black gooey stuff that I had seen so often in my many adventures. It bubbled and boiled like Jell-O gone berserk, great spouts of it shooting out into the air before being sucked back in.

It grew and grew as we flew closer. Soon it took up my whole vision, and I lost the ability to discern the features of the handsome face as it got too big. Except for the eyes. We flew straight toward them and then veered to the right eye.

It loomed before us, growing until all I could see was a flat expanse of black goo, any curvature lost in its sheer size. The Ka did not slow down.

Just before we slammed into the eye, the Ka reared to a stop like a horse, pulled me back with its huge arms, and slung me toward the wall of blackness.

With a great sucking sound, I entered the Stomper nightmare.

CHAPTER 55

Dirty Hand

Everything around me exploded, devouring all five of my senses. My ears were slammed with a barrage of terrible screams and wailing agony and rushing wind and clanking metal and breaking glass. Things touched my skin—wet things, sharp things, slithering things. Unbearable smells invaded my nose until I could taste them as well—sewage, rotten cabbage, body odor, bad breath. It all flew at me and around me and through me like a swarm of ghostly wasps.

But the worst part was what I could see.

Haunting visions of unspeakable things. Ghosts, demons, deformed animals, monsters—flashing glimpses of anything and everything that had ever terrified a child lying under his covers late at night. Things reached for me as the swirling vision of nightmares spun around and around me, speeding up and slowing down, flashing and disappearing, touching me, pulling me, pushing me.

I was in a tornado of horror.

And then I saw Half's face, floating in the madness.

"Go!" I screamed. "GO!"

"*Can you do it?*" he said back, although his lips didn't move.

"Just go!" I yelled through the storm of terror. "Just go!"

He disappeared.

The rage of nightmarish things picked up speed, turned into a torrent of rushing black wind filled with all the evil and cruelty and malice of the world.

And then it stopped without warning, gone completely.

My mind still spun, however, and I couldn't see anything. All I could feel was a hard floor supporting my feet below. Everything around me was dark.

I fell to the ground, and threw up.

I sat there for several minutes, spitting and wiping my mouth. My body shook as the terrifying images still played in my mind. I felt crippled and weak, like a child beat up one too many times by the school bully. The thought of my mom and dad and Rusty having to live through what I'd just seen, even for a second, made tears well up in my eyes. And deep down I knew it was only the beginning.

A few more minutes passed, the time helping me strengthen my resolve a little. As I sat, a faint light seemed to grow and illuminate my surroundings. I stood up when the picture became clear; then I shivered.

I was in a graveyard.

The light came from the moon, which had peeked out of a bank of clouds like a peeping tom. All around me, stretching away in all directions, was row after row of tall, ancient tombstones. They were straight from the scary cartoons of Halloween—leaning to one side, cracked and split, creepy, blackened letters proclaiming which unlucky person was dead and buried beneath.

Tendrils of mist flowed silently through the cemetery, parting to go around the tombstones like river water around a jutting rock. The white stuff gathered around my ankles like smoke and clung to my body. I kicked at it, making it billow and dissolve, only to be replaced by more.

A slight wind picked up, and I heard the soft rattle of leaves from a tree nearby. The breeze moaned as it blew through the tombstones, and then came the kicker.

An owl hooted.

I groaned out loud.

"Gimme a break," I said. "Is this the best that you can do?" I yelled out into the darkness. "This is your nightmare for me?"

It was then that a hand reached through the ground and grabbed my ankle.

CHAPTER 56

Zombies

I screamed and kicked my leg as hard as I could, breaking the hand's grip. It was green and moldy, the hand of a dead man. Shudders went through my body, and I stepped back a few steps, not taking my eyes off the thing. My thoughts spun, wondering why the Shield hadn't stopped the deathly fingers from touching me.

Another hand grabbed me. Yelling out, I kicked myself away from it too. Yet another hand burst through the ground to my right and then one to my left. An entire arm followed, and then a shoulder. I spun around, shaking with fear now. Hands and arms were everywhere, digging their owners out of the ground. My mind tried to tell me I was dreaming, but I knew it wasn't true. It wasn't the same. This was real, and every cell in my body felt it.

And the Shield. It hadn't worked.

Such simple words couldn't do it justice. The Shield, the thing that had protected me from so much, had failed me. The one thing that was supposed to make all of this bearable was not there—I could feel its absence.

212

I walked backward, looking all around at the army of zombies breaking from their earthy homes. I bumped into one, and spun around. Lifeless eyes stared at me, and a gaping hole for a mouth tried to smile.

I lost it.

Screaming, I ran. I didn't know which direction to go, and I didn't care. Stepping on and over bodies, pushing them aside, I slapped and hit at anything that came close to me. Dead fingers grabbed my shirt, decayed bodies converged in my path, trying to stop me. Adrenaline exploded in my system, and I steamed ahead, bulldozing everything out of my way. The only thing on my side was the fact that dead people don't have much strength.

But as I ran, I had another thought. Maybe they weren't supposed to be strong enough to get me. Maybe it was all part of how the Stompers worked—do just enough to scare the wits out of you but let you keep going from one nightmare to another.

As much as I tried to convince myself that was true, it didn't help much. My skin crawled with the heebie-jeebies, and my body shook even as I ran.

Straight ahead I went, like a raging warthog who's spotted some food, weaving in and out of the countless tombstones. I pushed zombies out of the way, left and right. Their bodies were light and frail as if they were made of papier-mâché. But the sight of their dead eyes and rotting skin and lipless grins was enough to haunt me for the rest of eternity. I kept running.

Up ahead, a light post appeared. It was black metal, tall, with a glass-encased candle burning at its top. It made no sense where it stood, in the middle of an upturned grave. Because I could see no end to the sea of tombstones and dead bodies,

I made for the post, running as hard as possible through the tangle of arms and groping hands. Five feet before I reached the light post, a body fell at my feet, tripping me. I flung forward headfirst, falling toward the soft earth.

I hit the ground, inches from the post. Dozens of zombies fell on top of me. Terrified beyond feeling, I reached forward and touched the cool metal.

Everything around me shattered apart, and I flew into a world of swirling, splitting colors.

CHAPTER 57

Airplane

Chaotic lights mixed with blackness spun around me, and my head felt like it would explode. My body twisted into weird shapes, and pain shot through my every part. Haunted shapes appeared again—ghouls and goblins, vampires and werewolves. I closed my eyes but somehow could still see the terrifying images.

And then, once again, it stopped on a dime.

I was in a bright place, but I squeezed my eyes shut as I clutched my stomach, trying my best to prevent another puking episode. Several minutes passed as I got control of things and tried to understand where I was.

I was lying on cold steel, and a terrible vibrating sound was accompanied by the loud hum of engines. When my vision adjusted a bit, I could see that I was in the main section of a huge cargo plane, the rattle of turbulence making everything shake. There were boxes and junk everywhere, most of it strapped down.

I stood up, and paused while my head swam. I didn't know what I had been expecting when I finally met the Stompers, but I wouldn't have guessed zombies and airplanes.

I walked around, trying to get a clue to my new location. None of the boxes were marked, and there was no rhyme or reason to anything on the plane. The slight jiggle of the whole thing as I walked around didn't help my stomach problems at all. Then I realized that someone must be flying the big piece of junk.

I ran toward the cabin up front, dodging the odds and ends scattered around the plane in no order or plan whatsoever. The door to the cockpit was closed, and I pulled up short just as I was about to tear it open. *What could be in there?* I thought. *This has to be a nightmare, just like the graveyard. Do I dare open it?*

After another few moments of hesitation, I reached down, pushed the metal lever, and swung the door open.

A man sat in the captain's chair, hands resting on the steering wheel or whatever they call the thing on an airplane. He turned and looked at me with a smile. He was ordinary in every sense—brown hair, six feet tall, neither fat nor skinny, slightly tanned skin. I had been expecting a monster, so seeing a nice airline pilot was a huge relief.

"Hey," I said, "where are we? Do you know what's going on—why I'm here?"

His smile never left his face. "Of course I do." He turned back to look out the windshield.

I waited a second, expecting him to continue. "So . . . can you tell me?" I finally asked.

Without looking at me, he said, "You've been very bad, Jimmy Fincher. Your little trick with the Dream Warden was not very nice at all." He laughed. "I will say this, however: those Givers sure come up with some clever ploys, don't they?"

Every bit of hope I'd gained, however small, ran away like vegetarians from a meat packing plant.

"What . . . who are you?" I asked.

"Why do you ask such stupid questions?" was his reply, the man still not looking at me.

"Are you a Stomper?"

"You're getting dumber, not smarter."

"Then just tell me!" I yelled. "Why am I here? Who are you?"

He laughed again. "You're here because they plan to destroy you with an unleashing of fear the likes of which has never been done before."

I didn't know what to say to that. For one of the few times in my life, I was speechless.

"You'd do well to give up now, Jimmy," he said to the window in front of him. "Even if you were to do the impossible and survive what lies ahead of you, then something even worse would happen. Better for you to die, my friend, than for you to cause the destruction of an entire world."

"What are you talking about?"

"You'll find out soon enough. But time has run out for now." He finally turned to face me. Everything about him was different—his skin was pale and covered in hives, his hair greasy, sweat covering his face. And his eyes were coal black.

"You see, this plane is going to crash in three minutes."

Before I could respond, the pilot disappeared.

He was gone—into thin air, no trace that he'd ever been there.

The plane jolted hard, throwing me forward. My head slammed into the back of the pilot's chair, and I fell backward onto the floor. The reality of losing the Shield hit me in that moment, and panic exploded throughout my body.

The Shield—why don't I have the Shield?

I got up, holding onto anything I could to keep steady. The plane was shaking badly now, bouncing up and down like a skateboard on rough gravel. I held the chair with tight fingers and looked through the windows. The plane was in the middle of dark gray clouds, and bolts of lightning exploded all around it, every two or three seconds.

One big bolt flashed and the plane rocked hard to the right, throwing me off my feet again. I scrambled over to the pilot's chair and fell into it. I could hear thunder and smelled something like fire. Grabbing the wheel, I tried to hold it steady while I looked around me at the jumble of controls. There was no way. Flying the plane to safety was not the way to get out of this mess.

I got back up and headed for the back, banging into things with every step. The plane was leaning toward the right in a constant, dizzying angle. Loud crashes boomed every second as I stumbled down the length of the plane. Horrible noises sent a million thoughts of terror through my head—bending metal and cracking plastic and shattering glass and weird popping sounds. I had no idea what to do. The only thing I could hope for was the light post at the cemetery—some kind of beacon, some kind of safety base. Could there be one on the plane?

The thought had barely finished processing through my brain when an entire section of the roof ripped off and vanished with an ear-piercing metallic scream. Like a speck of dust caught by a vacuum cleaner, I was sucked up out of the plane and into the raging storm.

CHAPTER 58

No Parachute

Wind and rain tore at me and it was impossible to tell which way was up or down as I tumbled over and over through the air. All was gray and wet and cold. After a while the shock of being ripped from the plane dissipated, only to be replaced by the fear of what came next. I fell toward the ground far below.

At first my heart felt like it was in my throat, but then I got used to it as I kept falling. I tried to keep myself in a still position, but the friction of the air kept turning me this way and that. My limbs were whipped in all directions by the wind. I calmed my mind as best I could and tried to come up with options. But nothing came.

I shot through the bottom of a cloud, and the browns and grays of the ground below came into view. It rushed up at me with alarming speed—I'd thought I would have more time. But I only had seconds left.

I righted myself a little so that my stomach faced the ground as much as possible, and after a couple of tries I was in the position of a normal skydiver. I searched everywhere for anything that could possibly be a light post but saw nothing but fields and trees, gray from the overhanging storm.

I was heading for a small clearing in the trees, and I knew landing would be the end of Jimmy Fincher. But then something popped into my head, and I couldn't believe it hadn't come earlier.

The Fourth Gift. The Power.

Ever since Farmer had given it to me, without much explanation at all, I had hardly thought about it. I didn't get the usual lesson on how to use it, and I didn't understand what it did, anyway. So what good was it?

He said it was the power to control the Yumeka. But the Shield wasn't working, why would this one?

All of these thoughts flew through my head in a few seconds as the gravity sucked me toward a certain death. I had no choice but to reach deep down and use my new Gift.

I called upon the Power, and tried to bend the Yumeka to my will.

All I asked for was a soft landing.

I was ten feet from the ground when everything slowed to an almost standstill. The ground, which had been racing at me with a speedy vengeance, halted its approach and went from a blurry, onrushing wall of dirt and rock to something that seemed a pleasant jump or two away. My fall had stopped in an instant, and I found myself floating on the air like a feather.

A few seconds later my feet touched the ground with a light thump, and it was over.

For the first time, I caught a glimpse of what Farmer meant when he said that the Fourth Gift was the most powerful. It appeared I could do whatever I wanted in this place.

Rain fell with a steady downpour, drenching me from top to bottom. My heart had a hard time slowing after the fall from the airplane, and that odd feeling of "too close for comfort" kept swelling up inside me. Although I had just been through it, I couldn't believe what had happened. I thought for sure my blood pressure couldn't take any more excitement.

I walked through the soaked landscape, looking for something, anything that would help me know what to do next. As my feet trudged through the mud and slop, I thought about everything I'd been experiencing.

This is what the Stompers do, I thought. *They take things from your memory, things that they know will scare you to death, and then they act it out for you.* Or maybe it had nothing to do with memory—what person *wasn't* afraid of zombies and falling out of airplanes? I wondered if it stayed like this, episode after episode, nightmare after nightmare, or did some of them take longer amounts of time—more developed fear.

Fear. It was hard to comprehend, but the fear I felt was food to the Stompers. *Well,* I thought, *I hoped they were hungry, because I just gave them a feast.*

I rounded a grove of trees, and in the distance I saw another lamp post set on top of a small hill. It was exactly like the one in the cemetery. I broke into a run and headed straight for it. With each step, mud and water flew up into the air, splattering the backs of my legs. I went up the hill and made it to the metal post.

I wasn't so sure I wanted to touch it. The dreaded thought of another nightmare made me feel sick and hopeless. How was I going to get out of this? Did I have to experience a different nightmare for every person I had replaced here? Would it go on forever? One thing occurred to me that almost stopped my heart for good—maybe this was my fate. Maybe my whole purpose was to live the rest of eternity here so that everyone else could live their normal lives.

But no. If that were so, then what would be the purpose of the Power? There had to be a way, and I was determined to figure it out.

I reached forward to touch the metal. Just before I made contact, a hand grabbed my shoulder.

CHAPTER 59
Teacher

I whipped around, ready to fight.

It was Farmer.

"What . . . what are you doing here?" Never in a million years would I have expected him to show up now. Before, he'd only visited me inside one of the magic doors.

"Well, it's good to see you too, my friend," he said, his gentle smile a relief after all I'd been through. The rain soaked his gray hair and beard, and his overalls looked like it was high time for him to buy some new ones.

"Trust me, Farmer, it's *very* good to see you," I said, letting out a big sigh. "How did you get here?"

"This is still the Yumeka, no matter how much control over it the Stompers may have. I can get myself around, you know."

"Does that mean that when I went through all those doors, I was in the Yumeka?"

"You could say that."

"I don't think I'm ever going to understand how this whole thing works."

He laughed. "Oh, you will, trust me."

"Why doesn't the Shield work here?" I asked.

"You volunteered to come, remember?" he replied. "The Shield will not protect you here, I'm sorry to say. It would defeat the purpose of your mission, my boy. How have you sacrificed for the others—how could the Stompers accept that—if you did not have the chance of being affected by it?" He leaned back and looked at the dark clouds above, then back at me. "No, when you signed up for this, you signed up for the whole package."

"Then why does the Fourth Gift work?" I asked.

"Because you are using it in its proper element. I said you had to take upon yourself this battle fairly, not give in completely. The Shield is not for this fight—that was to get you here. The Power is all you need now. It puts you and the Stompers on the same level. This should be a war to remember."

"Okay, so what am I supposed to do?"

"You must fight the nightmares. There will be many more, Jimmy. Many more. As I told you in our previous meeting, it hurts me so much to know that you have to do this. But the Power—it is your hope. Learn it, feel it, embrace it. With this Gift, you can win every time. I'm so proud of you for figuring that out already."

"Yeah, you could've showed up a little sooner."

"I couldn't, Jimmy, I couldn't. You had to use it once on your own before I could come and help you."

I threw my arms up into the air. "Who makes all these rules?" I asked. "Didn't you come up with all the Gifts—can't you do whatever you want?"

"Even if I could, I wouldn't. It's a higher law, my son, and one day you'll grow to understand that."

So many times he'd answered this way—that it was for me to learn and to grow and to understand. He sounded like my parents.

"Okay, fine," I said. "So is that it? I go through a bunch of nightmares and then all the Stompers die and go away?"

"No, I'm afraid it's not that simple."

"What do you mean?"

"When you have won enough battles, they will realize they've lost the first phase of this war. But then it will get worse. They'll realize your world is lost to them, and they will grow desperate. They are evil, Jimmy, and so they will do something of the utmost evil when it reaches that point."

"What?" I asked, not really wanting the answer.

"They'll try to destroy your world once and for all."

"Destroy it?" I asked, puzzled. "How can they destroy the world—isn't this all just a glorified dream?"

Farmer's face grew serious, his eyebrows squeezing together. "A glorified dream? Jimmy, you really are lost if you look at this place in that way. The Yumeka is as real as anything in your waking world, I can assure you. It's a melding of dreams and reality, and they both affect the other."

"So how would they destroy the world?"

"By destroying the Yumeka for your world."

"But how?"

"They would destroy it's mind."

"It's mind?"

"Yes. Jimmy, every world is alive—living and breathing as you are. And its mind and heart, or what some might call its soul, is trapped in the Stomper's clutches just as much as you and everyone else."

"Well, it's just me, now."

Farmer tilted his head like what I said wasn't totally true. "That, too, is not so crystal clear. Their real freedom is dependent on you defeating the Stompers."

"Okay, so tell me what I need to do to prevent them from blowing up earth."

Farmer laughed. "Oh, they won't blow it up. They'll just make it die."

"How do I stop it?"

"You must find the soul of your world before they do."

"Find it? How do you find a soul?"

"In the Yumeka it will be something symbolic that only you will understand. Unfortunately, I don't know what that is. But in the end, it will be you against them, trying to find it."

"Why am I not surprised that you don't know what it is?"

"Because you're getting smarter and smarter. You're catching on."

"Very funny. What else do I need to know to beat them?"

"After you win—not *if*, after—we will meet again. But for now, that's it."

"Can't you tell me more about the Power?"

"It really has no limits, Jimmy. You'll figure it out." Farmer sighed and then rubbed his chin. "Now, one last thing before I go. I have to tell you something, now—something that isn't going to be easy for you."

"What do you mean?"

Farmer's eyes dropped and any trace of a smile vanished. "I've been telling you for a long time that the biggest surprise of all was still in your future."

"Yeah?" I asked, my curiosity killing me.

"Well, it's time for you to know everything. All of it."

"Good, it's about time." I'd always felt in the dark on so many things.

Farmer frowned. "When I'm done, you'll long for the days when you didn't know what I'm about to tell you." He rubbed his eyes and face with his hands, and sighed. "It's about the Layers. Where you are, right now, is only another Layer of the Stomper's horrors. The Second Layer."

He leaned forward and his eyes narrowed.

"Jimmy, you have been inside the Yumeka for longer than you think—since before we even met. Since *before* the door in the woods."

CHAPTER 60

The Second Layer

"What?" I asked. Panic filled me as the first glimpses of understanding settled in.

"Please, hear me out. You know it in your heart, so don't fight it." He leaned back. "You and your family were captured and imprisoned by the Stompers almost a year ago. That was the First Layer, where you were subjected to all kinds of terrors and nightmares. It was in the recent months that the Stompers decided to go to the next Layer, the Second Layer. Your memories were wiped clean up to the point where they first invaded your world, and in your minds, inside the Yumeka, inside the clutches of the Stompers, you started all over."

My jaw dropped farther to the ground with every word out of his mouth. Bile rose up from my stomach, and I had to swallow it back down.

"Soon your memories will return," he continued. "You'll realize how different it was when they vanquished your world the first time. You see, the Blackness is not a gateway between physical planets, it is a gateway connecting the many worlds of the Yumeka. Yours and countless others. The only reason you were spared for so long is because of the lack of an actual iron gateway to Earth. In the end, the Black Curtain was the only way to get here. And that is the one mystery we may never understand."

"But," I said, my mind spinning, trying to come up with the right questions. "But, the Shadow Ka . . ."

"You would never have seen the Ka in their hideous form in your physical world. They came through the Ripping of the Curtain, entered the minds of those they could most easily conquer—people like Custer Bleak. They became Shadow Ka themselves, taking control of the Yumeka for your people, one by one using their power to pull people into the Black Coma.

"What you witnessed then was a blackening of the skies, people running around in chaos, holding their heads, fighting the song of the Shadow Ka in their minds and dreams. But eventually you lost, all of you, every last human sucked into the Black Coma and taken to the Stompers inside the Yumeka. Those humans possessed by the Ka have spent their lives since taking care of your bodies—literally feeding them and keeping them alive.

"When you finally win this war, your people will wake up, finding a world that is decayed and rotting. It will take many years to rebuild, but recover they will.

"But until then, your real bodies will remain in that coma, lying wherever they may be in the physical world. Yours is probably getting very hungry since you sent the Ka through the Black Curtain. You must get back soon before you starve to death."

As Farmer spoke and shattered my whole perception of the life I'd lived and the world around me, my mind grew numb and my stomach ill. It was way too much information to process fully, but the gist of it had hit home, and hit hard. Everything I'd done—the Doors, the battles, the rescues—all of it had been done within the confines of the Yumeka, inside the fabricated world of the Stompers.

"So . . . this past year has been a dream?" I asked, staring at an empty spot in the gray distance.

"A dream?" asked Farmer. "My dear boy, this is not a dream. I've told you before, the Yumeka is just as real as the physical world. It's just . . . different."

"Why didn't you tell me before?" I asked.

"I couldn't. Believe me when I tell you that it was difficult. But I couldn't. The whole essence of your battle with the Shadow Ka in the First Layer was defeating them within what their masters had created. It could not have worked any other way. We spent centuries looking and planning for such an opportunity. And you did it, Jimmy—you did it. And now that you are in the Second Layer, you are ready for the truth."

My head sunk toward the soggy ground. It was almost too much to handle. In the real world I was lying somewhere in a coma? I'd been trapped within the Yumeka for a year? It was just too much.

"But . . ." was all I could get out.

"Jimmy, this changes nothing but your perception of the past. The future is still in your hands. If you defeat the Stompers in any Layer, you win. You'll wake up inside the Yumeka, free from your enemy, tell your loved ones the truth, and then everyone will be ready to wake up in the real world. Yes, you'll be a little older than you think, but what does that matter? You'll have won, and it will be over."

"What does it matter?" I asked, tears welling up in my eyes. "To be told that you're living a lie? That the past year of your memory is something planted there by evil creatures? To know that my real body is lying on some stone bed somewhere, hoping to one day wake up? I think it matters a lot."

"I know, it's hard to accept," Farmer said. "But when it's over, and you do get your life back, I promise you—all will be right in the world."

I fell to the ground, mud and water soaking me instantly, and put my head in my hands. "Just leave me alone," I said. "I need to think."

"Okay, Jimmy. Take your time, but remember what you must still do." He walked away to a nearby tree and leaned against it. "I won't leave," he yelled through the rain, "until you are ready to move ahead. Think on things, and come to terms with it."

My mind spun trying to take it all in. Everything I could remember of the past year was part of the nightmares of the Stompers—a plan to put me in a position where they could suck the fear out of me from the very beginning all over again. I knew nothing about the real world and what awaited me there if I was able to get back. It made me hurt inside, and for a long time I sat and pondered Farmer's revelation.

I finally stood up, and told him to come back. He walked over.

"Just tell me one thing," I said, "and I want the truth."

"Anything."

"Is my family, and my home, and all that—is that just made up?"

"No, Jimmy, no. The Stompers can only do so much. The basic structure of your lives before they came—especially your families—are all duplicated here. Back in your real life, there is your mom and dad, and Rusty. There is Duluth, Georgia.

Most of your memories are real—up until the day the Shadow Ka came. That I promise you."

"Then I'm ready."

Farmer pointed to the lamp post. "Good. You have much to accomplish."

"Thanks for the help." I didn't disguise my sarcasm at all. "All I have to do is go through a bunch of nightmares within one big nightmare that I've been living for a year and then find the soul of a whole planet before the bad guys do. No problem. See ya."

"Wait," Farmer said. "Jimmy, wait." He paused for a minute. "I want you to know that everything has been for a purpose. I'm glad it's you here, at this time, when everything comes to an end. If I could do this for you . . ."

"Farmer, don't worry about it, I mean it. I can do this. Don't worry about me."

"I know you can do it, Jimmy. I know it. Now go."

Without another word, he reached behind him and grabbed at the air. A Ripping of the Black Curtain opened up, although I couldn't see what was on the other side. He winked, stepped through, and was gone. With its usual sound of static electricity and ripping paper, the opening closed.

Soaked to the bone and miserable, still shocked from all that Farmer had told me, I turned to the lamp post and touched it.

CHAPTER 61

Next

The same swirling chaos of color and terrifying images consumed me, and I spun out of that place. The nausea and fear crept back into my system, and I tried my best to close my eyes. But it did no good. I could still see everything.

I couldn't do this every time. It was driving me insane. I called upon the Power with my mind, reaching out to the madness around me and trying to make it stop. Nothing happened. There was only spinning color and blackness and images of the dead. Not specific enough, I thought. I tried again, this time telling it to stop spinning. It stopped. Everything was still the same, but there was no motion. It was a start.

I didn't have much time to enjoy it, because it all went away a few seconds later, and I entered the next nightmare of the Stompers.

This time I was in a big lake.

It was huge, so that I could hardly see the banks on both sides of me. I treaded water right in the middle, the dark brown water surrounding me like dirty chocolate milk. It looked and felt filthy, and I began swimming. I didn't know where I was going or why, but I had to get moving.

Something whipped past my leg, bumping it.

I cried out and kicked underneath the water. It connected with something solid that swam away. Shuddering at the thought of what could be under there, I swam a little faster. I tried my best to keep the water out of my mouth, but bits of it kept trickling in. Nausea had been my constant friend lately, and it came back in full force. The water tasted foul.

I swam on.

Another thing bumped my leg. Then another. I kicked out both times and kept swimming. The shore wasn't getting any closer.

Something sharp nicked my leg. Then a big mouth closed around my right shoe, teeth digging into my flesh. I kicked my foot out and thrashed my legs in every direction, panic beginning to overwhelm me. The water churned all around me as more of the creatures came to play.

I couldn't take it anymore. Calling upon the Power, I threw my thoughts into pushing the things away. Water swirled as the Gift pushed the creatures away from me, displacing large chunks of the lake, only to have it fill right back up. I couldn't get a good look at the creatures, but slimy bodies kept bumping and nipping me. I concentrated on the Power as I swam, and everything became difficult to manage.

Still not sure what I was doing, I told the Power to pick me up and take me to shore. I flew out of the water and bumped along the top of it as some unseen force dragged me across the lake. I tried to bring it under control but my mind couldn't focus. Slapping and skimming the lake's surface, I flew toward shore, leaving the *things* far behind. But my body got decorated with bruises as I went.

When I reached the shore, the force threw me off the lake. I tumbled along the sand until I smashed into a tree. I rolled over onto my back and groaned. Every inch hurt, and my head spun. I had a lot to learn about using the Power.

A hundred yards or so down the shore of the lake was another lamp post. With all of my heart I wanted to stop—it sickened me to think of going through more of these nightmares. But I pushed forward, knowing there was no other choice. I had to do this, and do it until something changed. My one hope was the Power. Once I got it under control, things would get easier.

As I neared the post, I almost laughed thinking of Farmer and his lessons where he made me raise my arms. We hadn't gotten that far this last time, and maybe that was why it was so difficult.

Thoughts of his revelation about the last year of my life sobered me right up.

I made it to the post, and without hesitating, touched it.

From there I went to an insane asylum where some crazed killers chased me around until I figured out I could just flick them away with the Power every time they got close to me. It didn't take long to find another lamp post.

Then it was a school bus, out of control, driving down the wrong side of the freeway. I sat in the back, and there wasn't any sign of a driver or passengers. I fought myself, pushing away the panic, and turned to the back door of the bus. I opened it, and jumped out, using the Power to make me land nice and easy. I ran to the side of the road and found a lamp post. That one had been way too easy, I thought, and figured it was because I didn't do what it expected—stay on the bus and freak out the whole time.

I touched the post.

From there it went on and on.

Burning buildings, bank robberies, trapped in a buried coffin. Each time, I learned more and more about the Power and how to use it. Earthquakes, tornadoes, exploding volcanoes. Meteors, hurricanes, and tidal waves. Nightmare after nightmare, the Stompers went for my fear.

But each time, I won.

And then the next phase began.

CHAPTER 62

Mansion Again

Something was different about this new place. I couldn't put my finger on it, but there was something very different.

I stood on a long paved driveway, with huge trees lined along its edges. The season was late fall because the trees had lost most of their leaves and they covered the ground. It was daytime, but there's wasn't much light, and the sky was cloudy and gray. A soft breeze blew leaves up and around me, their crinkling sound reminding me so much of fall evenings with my family.

The driveway led to an old house, at least eighty feet away from where I stood. It looked like an old plantation—its huge porch with pillars welcoming me for a visit. The house had once been white, but years of neglect had left it gray and ugly. Shutters were torn, debris was everywhere, and a couple of windows were broken. It looked for all the world like a haunted house.

Which meant I was supposed to enter it.

Now that I had more confidence in the Fourth Gift, and didn't want to waste any more time, I walked toward the house.

Crunch, crunch, crunch went the leaves with every step as I got closer to the steps leading to the porch. Except for the breeze and the leaves, there was no sign of movement or life anywhere.

I scanned the area as I walked, trying to anticipate things jumping out at me or whatever. But nothing happened.

I reached the steps, climbed them, and walked up to the front door. The porch was empty—not even a chair or wind chimes or anything. Definitely a haunted house, I thought. The door was old and pockmarked, with its paint long gone, replaced by dirt and grime. The handle was rusted and bent to the side. I grabbed it and gave the door a push.

It swung inward with a loud creak.

Come on, people, I thought. *Come up with something original.*

The inside was very dark, but I could make out the shadows of a staircase and some furniture. From somewhere in the back, a light shone. I walked toward it, every step letting out a loud, wooden groan. Maybe this nightmare was a simple case of falling through rotting wood and being attacked by rats. But the floor held up under my weight.

I went down a small hallway, around a couple of bends, and then saw the room where the light came from. It flickered against the walls of the hallway, so I knew it must be some kind of fire. How cozy.

Bracing myself mentally, readying my mind to use the Power at any moment, I entered the room.

This one differed from the rest of the house in every way. There was no dust, no cobwebs, no worn-out furniture— everything looked in pristine condition. There were a fancy couch and chairs, elaborate drapes on the window, paintings of old people on the walls, and a nice roaring fire in a stone fireplace. The carpet was thick and plush, and one wall was covered by a bookcase, filled with leather-bound books. It was the sitting room straight out of those movies my mom liked.

Except for one small difference.

In the chair by the fireplace sat a monster.

CHAPTER 63

Weird Thing in a Chair

❧❧

I barely had time to register what the thing looked like. It was green, with horns, and there was something very strange about its feet. But then it shifted into something else—a big hairy thing that looked like Bigfoot. Seconds later it changed again—this time into a slimy alien with two humongous eyes. Then it was a skeleton, then a mummy, then a witch, then a big blob of red goo. When it turned into a Stormtrooper, I'd had enough.

"Cut it out!" I yelled. "You're not scaring me one bit."

It changed again, this time into a human male, dressed in a nice black suit with a vest. He had slicked-back hair, was chubby, and puffed away at a cigar.

"Who are you supposed to be?" I asked.

"Huh?" he asked in a weird accent, holding his hands up like I must be the dumbest kid in the world. "You don't recognize me?"

"Never seen you before in my life," I said, rolling my eyes.

"I'm Al Capone, you idiot."

"Great, what do you want, Al?" I asked.

"You smart-aleck kid." He reached behind him and pulled out an old-fashioned machine gun. Then he stood up. He pressed the trigger and bullets exploded out of it in a swarm.

I held my hand up and flicked it to my right. The Power swept the bullets away with a quick swoosh and they slammed into the nice paintings on the wall. One got an old king-looking dude right between the eyes.

"Ha!" yelled Capone. "Nice work! You're getting handy with that thing."

"Just tell me what's going on."

The man changed again, this time into a tall woman with long black hair. She wore a red, flowing dress, and her skin was as white as Casper the Friendly Ghost.

"I see you are one who realizes when the situation is grave," she said, her voice soft but steady.

"Who or what are you?"

She sat down, smoothing her dress, and then crossed her legs. Her eyes were black, and they fixed on mine.

"I am the Blade of the Stompers."

"The Blade?"

"Yes. Their leader, their spokesperson, whatever you want to call it."

"What's different about this place?" I looked around. "When does the nightmare start?"

"Those are over, young man. Although it pains me to admit it, you've beaten us in that regard. Of course, you will regret doing so."

The conversation was making me uncomfortable. For one thing, she didn't seem evil enough to represent the Stompers. And the way she talked about things . . . it was so nonchalant, like none of this really mattered.

It was a trick. All of it. The Stompers were wasting my time on purpose.

"Lady, tell me right now where the soul of the world is."

She laughed.

Throwing the Power at her, I lifted her into the air and curled her into a ball. As she hovered, I squeezed her neck with the invisible force. She thrashed about and sputtered, trying to stop the choking.

"You fool," she said, her words a painful whisper. "They're already searching—you'll never make it."

I released the Power. With a loud thump she crashed onto the carpet, her limbs splaying all over the place.

"What're you talking about?" I yelled at her.

She righted herself into a sitting position and then glared at me.

"Your selfishness—your unceasing selfishness has only made it worse," she said. "Now, instead of life, they will all die with your world. All of them."

"You call this life?" I screamed, throwing her back against the wall with the Power. "Every one of us would choose death if it was the only other choice."

"Then you have chosen for them," she said.

"No, you're wrong." I said. "I choose life."

With an explosion of the Power, I blew the lady and the house away into oblivion.

It was time to start searching.

CHAPTER 64

Shadow

The shattered remains of the house lay in pieces all around me. There was no sign of the lady, but I knew she wasn't real and had probably just disappeared. Wasting no time, I looked around for a lamp post. I knew of no other way to get around in the strange dreamscape of the Stompers.

I walked away from the rubble and back down the long driveway. Searching the land left and right revealed nothing but fields and trees, and soon it was too dark to see anyway. I reached the end of the drive where it intersected with a country road barely wider than the one I was on. A tall wooden post stood there with an electric light at its top, shining brightly.

I ran to it and touched it with both hands, but nothing happened. Disappointment filled me. It wasn't the right kind of light post, I reckoned.

I looked down the road both ways but saw nothing in either direction beyond the outer reaches of the light. I stood in a bubble of light surrounded by darkness, and had no idea what to do.

Talk about finding a needle in haystack. And to make matters worse, I had no idea how big the haystack was, or what the needle looked like. This was a mess.

The Power. There had to be a way to use the Power to help in the search.

I sat on the pavement and put my mind to work. It was almost scary to mess around with the Fourth Gift because of its unlimited capacity to do whatever I could conjure up. But then again, it had to have *some* limits. I tried making it just get rid of the Stompers altogether, but that didn't work. It seemed to only work when I could think of tangible, specific commands for it.

I tried another approach, telling it to bring the soul of the world to me.

Nothing.

Frustrated, I lay down on my back and looked at the sky. There were no stars and no moon—only clouds. Thoughts drifted in and out of my head, but nothing that was of any use. After a while, I started to drift away into sleep. I shook it off and stood up. Telling myself that I was already asleep and didn't need to waste time doing it here, I did some jumping jacks to wake myself up.

It was then that I noticed the large shadow standing at the edge of the light.

A shiver went down my spine, and then I almost fainted when the thing started walking toward me.

It came into the light, and just as it did, dozens of other shapes came into view behind it. They were all big, they were all black, and they all had wings.

Shadow Ka.

I couldn't believe it. I had been so sure that I was done with these guys for good, and yet here they were again, ready to torment me. Well, I didn't have time for it. I lifted my hand, ready to blow them to another country with the Power.

"Wait!" a voice screamed, a human voice. I dropped my hand.

From behind the first Ka a figure stepped forward, a man. When the light hit his face, I gasped out loud.

It was the man from under Mount Fuji—the guy who'd taken my offer and abandoned his Shadow Ka ways. Sato was his name. But I was at a complete loss to think how he could be there with me.

"How . . ." I didn't even finish the question, I was so confused.

"Let me explain," he said, holding his hands up. "It's a long story. But first you need to know one thing."

"What's that?" I asked.

"We're here to help you. All of us."

CHAPTER 65

Piggyback

"Why didn't you get sent through the Black Curtain?" I asked. "And how did you follow me here?"

"Follow you here?" he asked, looking confused. "That was the easy part—you must not understand everything yet."

"Yeah, tell me about it."

"The reason we didn't get sent to your battle with the other Ka, and then to the Blackness—that's another story."

"What happened?"

"Well, after you convinced us that day to abandon the Ka, we were hopeless and destitute. Our hearts had no life in them, and we came close to giving up altogether. A huge pack of Ka came after us, ready for their revenge, but then they were swept away in a great wind, gone in seconds. We were in our human form then, so it didn't take us. That's the only explanation I can come up with."

"Maybe it's because you had abandoned the Ka in your hearts," I said. "Even though physically you're still Ka. I don't know—I'm not the expert on all this junk."

"Whatever the reason, we soon knew that something

248

amazing had happened. Everywhere around us, people woke up. We couldn't believe it—it seemed impossible. I still don't understand fully what you've done. But when I found out that you were here, in this battle all alone—I knew we had to come. I don't know what we can do—but we will die trying if we have to."

"But why do you want to help me?"

"Because you gave us the courage to take our lives back. I'm sorry we didn't appreciate it when we first met, but we're here now, ready to thank you in the best way we know how."

I didn't know what to say—things sure seemed to make me speechless lately.

"But . . . how did you get *here?*" I finally asked.

Again he looked confused, but then he shook it off. "Remember who we used to serve, Jimmy. Just accept it— we're here, ready to fight."

"I don't need fighters," I said. "I need help finding something."

Sato broke into a smile, the first time I'd seen him do so.

"Trust me," he said. "We know how it works. Yes, you need to find something. But if you don't think you'll need to fight in order to find it, you've got another thing coming."

"Good point," I said.

"Come," he said. "Climb on my back. We need to find the Stompers. Wherever they are, that's where we should be looking."

As soon as the last word was out of his mouth, he morphed into a full-blown Shadow Ka. He pointed to his back with one of his huge claws.

Shaking my head at the craziness of it all, I climbed onto his back and wrapped my arms around his huge neck and shoulders. He helped hoist me up with the tops of his wings, and I settled into position, my legs resting on the place where the wings joined his back. I closed my eyes and asked myself if I was ready to trust this guy.

Before I could finish the thought, he whipped his wings out and we shot off into the air.

We rocketed into the sky so quickly that my stomach seemed to stay behind on the ground. The Ka's wings didn't flap as much as normal—it was almost like they were spaceships or airplanes. I figured it must have something to do with being in the Stompers' dreams, and concentrated on just trying to hold on.

Because of the dark night, I couldn't see much as we flew. The pack of Shadow Ka stayed in a tight group, and we flew for hours. I dozed off several times, only to find myself jerked awake by the horrible sensation of slipping off the Ka. Later, I slept for quite some time, and when I woke up I realized the Ka's massive claws were holding my arms so I wouldn't fall. It was still hard to see these guys as allies, but I was grateful.

Dawn had hit the world while I was snoozing, and it was a relief to finally see daylight again. The sky had cleared for the most part, and the taint of the Ka was weak—so it actually looked like a beautiful day. I couldn't remember the last time I'd seen that.

There was nothing below us but an empty wasteland—it reminded me of the desert Hairy drove me through on the way to that lake where Dad saved me from the Blackness. All I could see were endless stretches of dirt and gangly shrubs and red rock. I tried to pull my hand from the grip of the Ka to scratch my nose, but he wouldn't let me.

That's weird, I thought.

I pulled harder, and his claws tightened around me.

"Hey, what are you doing?" I yelled over the wind and flapping wings. "I have to scratch—do you mind?"

The Ka screamed, and I knew something was terribly wrong.

Then I noticed the chains.

CHAPTER 66

Deceived

❦

Since I'd woken up, I hadn't moved much because I was taking in all the new sights. But the Ka's strange reaction made me squirm and kick, panic flooding through me. When I moved my body, I heard a loud clanking sound at the same time I realized something was restraining my movements. I tilted my head at a weird angle to see my body.

I was completely wrapped in thick metal chains.

Then I understood. These were not Ka. They were parts of yet another nightmare.

I couldn't believe I'd been so stupid to trust anything in that place. I decided right then that I wasn't going to waste any time chatting with the Ka anymore. It was time to use the Power.

But before I could form another thought, the Ka holding me screamed and dove for the desert below, the rest of his pack following. There was no warning or gradual descent—we shot to the ground like we'd been blown out of a cannon. The sudden speed and change of direction sent my head spinning and my stomach turning. Wind tore at my face and my chained body lifted off of the Ka's back, his grip on my arm the only thing keeping me attached.

My body slammed against his back and then up into the air again, over and over. They weren't using their wings— those were folded behind them—and their heads and bodies pointed straight below. As I banged about I caught glimpses of the other Ka around me. They looked like a rain of black arrows shooting toward the ground.

I squeezed my eyes shut and tried to recover my thoughts. I concentrated on the Power, trying to move past the confusion of the situation. Somewhere in the deep parts of my mind, I found it, and grabbed it with all my might.

With a quick thought, I blew the chains into a million pieces, its parts flying away from us in an instant. Then I grabbed the Ka's claws with my mind, and forced his fingers apart one by one. He screamed something awful but didn't stop his insane descent. The ground was close now, rushing up at us with alarming speed.

I got the last finger loose and started to drift away from him.

But then the other Ka attacked me, all at the same time.

I felt nails rip into my back, and something bit my leg. Dozens of clawed hands grabbed every part of my body as we plummeted downward, attacking me like some nightmarish, living mobile. I threw the Power out in all directions, and it ripped the Ka away. An instant later others replaced them, grabbing and clawing and biting. I blasted them away. Again, others replaced them.

In the corner of my eye I saw the ground, and it was all yellow.

I had to switch gears, throw my mind's efforts into breaking the fall. Just like when I fell from the airplane, I used the Power to stop me, and I came to a sudden and complete standstill, hovering several feet from the odd-colored patch of ground below us. The second I stopped, the Ka holding me slammed away from me and into the ground. But instead of lots of black splats, the Ka were swallowed into the yellow dirt, like boulders falling into thick lava.

I was just trying to understand what happened when a pack of Ka grabbed every limb of my body, and before I could think up a reaction, they carried me into the yellow abyss.

As one we were swallowed—sucked into the earth.

CHAPTER 67

Yellow Goo

Thick, grainy liquid covered every inch of my skin. I closed my mouth too late, and swallowed a big glob of the stuff, making my stomach wrench. I puked it out, only to have more come in, gagging me. The clawed hands of the Ka gripped me tighter, carrying me farther and farther into the earth. The only sounds I could hear were the swooshing and the sucking of the . . . quicksand.

It was quicksand.

Down, down we went, the stuff getting thicker and thicker. I held my breath and knew that my heart wouldn't last much longer. My whole chest hurt, begging for air. The chaos and panic made it so hard to think. But I had to—I had to.

I forced myself to calm down and quit struggling. Then I unleashed the full power of my Gift.

The Ka exploded away from me and a huge air pocket formed in the quicksand. I was completely surrounded on all sides by yellow goop. I fell to the bottom of the bubble and there was a big *slurp* as my feet sunk into the yucky stuff. I looked upward, only knowing the direction by what my senses told me. Ka were ripping through the bubble now, trying their best to get back at me.

But I was done with them.

I pointed my hands to the sky above, and the Power blasted me upward.

The force of the Gift ripped me through the yellow dirt and grime, parting it as I went up, until a few seconds later I burst out of the quicksand and flew up into the air. I was filthy, and as the Power lifted me far away from the sinking pool and set me down on a huge rock, I tried to wipe myself clean. The stuff reeked, making me gag.

I landed on a rock and bent over to spit as much of the quicksand out of my mouth as possible. I kept my eye on the spot I'd just exited, expecting the Ka to come after me at any second. But they never came. It hit me then that those things hadn't been Shadow Ka at all but just figments of the Stomper dreamscape. It made me sick inside, and I wondered what really happened to those guys from the cave.

I looked around, knowing that it was too quiet—that something awful had to happen soon.

And I was right.

From far to my left, an army of . . . *things* were marching toward me. They were huge, made of metal and stone and clay, thrown together at odd angles with patchwork construction. Some were two-armed, two-legged robot-looking monsters, like something out of an old science fiction magazine. Others were deformed heads rolling along on big wheels. Some looked like boxes with legs coming out. There were dozens of others, and I didn't want to find out anything more about them.

I turned to go the other direction—to my right.

But from there came an army of a different sort.

Marching straight toward the spot where I stood were a bunch of dinosaurs. T-rexes mainly, big and vicious with short arms and sharp teeth. That didn't seem like much fun at all. So I looked straight ahead, the only direction that didn't lead back into the quicksand.

The ground was . . . *moving* over there. It was like the dirt and rocks had turned into gray matter, swaying and shifting back and forth. Then I realized why.

They were snakes. And I didn't have to study one of them any closer to assume that they were very poisonous.

The Stompers were attacking me from all directions.

Then I noticed something way in the distance, behind the oncoming snakes.

Deep in the horizon there were two massive cloud formations, one to the far left, the other to the far right. There was a pinkish hue to the formations, and they billowed and churned like smoke from a fire. The two were converging together—it seemed like they were moving slowly from this distance, but it was probably a different story when you got closer. But they were on a definite path to meet at a point far ahead, through the snakes.

A memory slipped up from somewhere in the deep parts of my mind.

Something about the Stompers.

We had seen them coming through the great Ripping up in New York, but later Inori had described them to me in more detail. They were ghostlike, almost like mist when in their true form and up close, with a pinkish color to them. But from a distance . . .

From a distance they would look like clouds.

My stomach flipped inside, and my heart started dancing.

I knew what was happening. There could be only one reason for that many Stompers to abandon their nightmare form and head for a specific spot. Those two clouds were converging on one thing and one thing only. And if they met before I got there, it was over.

The Stompers had found the soul of the world.

CHAPTER 68

Take to the Skies

I reminded myself that everything in this place was symbolic, but that didn't make it any less important. Whatever represented the soul, whatever thing it was that if destroyed, meant that my world would die, was out there, I knew it. And if they got to it before I did . . .

I threw the thoughts away and jumped into action. I ran straight for the snakes.

I was dirty and tired, but a new burst of adrenaline brought me to full strength. I pounded across the dirt and rocks, watching my step as best I could but mostly running full force.

The sea of snakes slithered across the ground, all intent on one target—me. As I got closer, I could see their varied colors and shapes and fangs. I didn't know one type of snake from another any more than I could pick out patterns of fancy wallpaper, but they looked awfully bad to me.

I threw a stream of the Power ahead of me, clearing a path through the slithering sea like a shovel pushed through snow.

With hisses and spits, the snakes were thrown to my left and right, only to come back together behind me as I ran with all of my strength. I kept my eyes on the two storms of Stompers way up ahead, and they were getting closer and closer together. I only had minutes.

The snakes didn't faze me as I pushed myself forward, step by step. But the reality of how far I was from the Stompers sent a shiver of panic through me. I hadn't gotten much closer, but I could already see a difference in how quickly the two groups were moving toward each other. There was no way I could make it in time.

I wasn't using the Power to its full potential, but what else . . .

At that moment the snakes disappeared.

They were replaced by millions of swarming bees.

They were the killer kind—I'd seen a show on PBS about them. I had the horrible thought that it was exactly *because* I'd seen the TV show that they appeared. The Stompers used my mind to find things that would scare me.

And small flying things that can kill you with a quick touch definitely scared me.

I stopped running, and they flew in for the attack.

For just an instant I started to raise my hand to swat at them but immediately realized what an idiotic thing that would be. Instead I reached inside for the Power and exploded it outward, blowing away thousands of the pests with a wave of silent air.

But less than a second later the next group came at me.

They swarmed in, the buzzing almost worse than their sting. It was like pouring soda fizz down my ear canals, and it drove me crazy. I had to fight the urge to clamp my hands on my ears.

I blew them away. Another group came in, swarming and reaching for any spot of my skin. I threw more effort into the Power, this time vaporizing millions of the bees.

More came still.

Again and again and again I threw the force of the Power at the bees, and they came back every time. Hating to waste time, I turned and ran toward the distant clouds of Stompers, blowing bees away every other second with my Gift. It was tiring—I could feel my muscles weakening, even though it was my brain doing all the work. It was the same fatigue I'd experienced under Mount Fuji, and I could only hope that some deeper use of the Power would kick in just like the Ice had done.

I ran on, constantly ridding myself of the pests.

The Stompers up ahead had almost halved the gap between them since the first time I looked. To keep running was ridiculous—I needed either to give up or find another way.

If only I were Superman, I thought.

My stupidity alarm went off with the thought. There was no 'if' about it. In this place, I could be whatever I wanted.

I stopped running. Throwing a little extra effort into my next wave of bee-repelling Power waves, I blew away millions of the stingers to give myself just a few more seconds. As the next swarm came at me, only moments away, I closed my eyes and pictured in my head what I wanted.

Then I was ready.

After one more swat at the bees, I took a running start and jumped with all of my strength into the air, both hands pointing to the sky.

Like a rocket heading for the moon, I shot into the sky in an explosion of air and power.

CHAPTER 69

Soul Searching

I was flying, just like the Man of Steel.

The friction of the wind tore at my hair and made it hard to breathe. In seconds I was far above the ground. I organized my thoughts and put them to work controlling the flying power. My body leveled off and I headed straight for the place between the Stomper clouds, still miles away.

I let my arms fall back to rest by my side as I flew to save their strength—it was hard to hold them in front of me with the air beating against them. I felt a little disappointed that Superman wasn't very practical when he flew, but I quickly got over it.

Like a cruise missile I bulleted through the air. I could feel the gap between me and the Stompers closing now, and for the first time felt some hope. My mind wandered a bit, wondering what the object we all chased could be. Something that represented the soul of the world—a symbol that only I would truly understand. I increased my speed, more and more confident that I would make it in time.

But then things changed.

A black shape appeared in front of me, blocking my path. It had no discernible features at first but then coalesced into a misshapen, deformed version of a Shadow Ka. It was huge— three times the size of a normal Ka. I halted my flight and hovered in midair, staring, transfixed. Then the thing spoke.

"You didn't think I would give up, did you?"

It was Raspy. My hope faded as quickly as it had come.

"How did you get here?" I yelled.

"Get here? I'm the leader of the Shadow Ka, I can go wherever I want—enter any Layer I want."

"I don't have time for this," I said, realizing I'd already wasted valuable seconds. With a thought I resumed my flight, altering my course to go around Raspy.

His gaze followed me as I picked up speed. Just as I passed where he floated, his body exploded into thousands of pieces. Millions. They grew and formed into monstrous black birds with savagely sharp beaks, flapping their wings with psychotic urgency. As one they flew at me.

I ignored them, throwing all my energy into flying toward the merging Stompers. But seconds later they caught up and surrounded me, and then they dove in for the kill.

Like a cloud of bloodthirsty gnats they attacked my body. They nipped and snapped at my skin, biting and tearing. Pain shot through me, like acupuncture gone bad. I had to take some of my focus off flying and blow them away with the Power. But they came right back.

"You will die today," synchronized voices said, coming from the birds and yet not coming from them, a disembodied sound that I knew was Raspy. "I told you it would end this way."

The birds swarmed around me, attacking with increased ferocity. Despite my efforts with the Power, it was impossible to keep them away. They seemed to disintegrate and reappear like magic, always right next to my skin. I concentrated harder, worked harder, pushing them away with my every thought.

I realized too late that I had completely ceased flying, and the land below rushed up at me.

The birds vanished when my body slammed into the ground.

It was like liquid sand again, softening the blow of the landing, sucking me in. I pushed downward with the Power, forcing my body back up to the sky. Just as I broke the surface of the quicksand, something big and wet wrapped around my neck.

It was a tentacle, ten inches thick.

Another one grabbed and squeezed my leg; then two others got my arms. A fifth wrapped around my torso, pulling me into the ground.

"NO!" I screamed.

I used the Power to cut them all clean in half, thrashing my body, pushing and pulling the tentacles off me. More came and then even more. For every one I cut off, two more appeared out of the sand, grabbing me wherever they could. Down I went.

I paused, gathering my thoughts, holding my breath as once again I was surrounded in goop. I fought down the panic, telling myself that I couldn't let the fear win. I had to beat the terror. I had to stay focused.

With one precise thought, I obliterated each tentacle, and catapulted myself back to the sky, like I was shot from a cannon. Seconds later I was high above, safe. I looked to the pink clouds.

The Stompers had once again halved their distance to the soul of the world.

Raspy appeared again, even more deformed than before. His whole body was a blob of black goo, bubbling and churning, his features almost indiscernible.

"You are weak, Jimmy, weak!" he yelled. "You let me toy with you while my masters destroy everything you have ever loved. You are nothing!"

"Get out of my way," I said, readying myself to fly forward.

I kicked out a wave of force with the Power, destroying Raspy once and for all. My body shot toward the Stompers.

Custer Bleak's last statement before he ceased to exist came like a whisper in my ears.

"I give you to my masters."

The Stompers unleashed all the furies of their evil.

Out of nowhere, from all directions, came hundreds and thousands of demons and beasts and monsters. Every horror book I'd ever read, every scary movie I'd ever seen, every terrifying story I'd ever heard, whether truth or fiction— anything and everything that was dark in my mind came flying at me with a terrible vengeance.

Flying vampires tried to bite me. Werewolves tried to rip my limbs off. Trolls and goblins threw rocks and clubs at my body. Orcs shot a rain of arrows with poison-laced tips. Each and every time I called on the Power to push them away.

I flew on, screaming with the effort of defending myself against the evil hordes while still flying as fast as possible.

Airplanes appeared, equipped with guns and bombs, firing at will. Blades and swords flew at me, although I couldn't see who threw them. Boogeymen and witches and warlocks and vicious dogs and chainsaws and masked men and serial killers and sharks and balls of roaring fire and lightning and flying spikes.

They all came at me, ripping and roaring and tearing and exploding. There were screams and shrieks and bloodcurdling cries. The world around me had turned into a complete and living nightmare. I flew on, crying from the horror of what surrounded me. Nothing—nothing in my entire life had been so terrible. The evil of it all squeezed my soul, and ripped every last ounce of joy from my heart.

But I flew on. For Mom. For Dad. For Rusty. For everyone.

I threw the Power of the Fourth Gift at the nightmares with one last, concentrated push. There was a millisecond where everything grew quiet, and the nightmares around me froze in midair. Then a silent clap of thunder exploded away from me like the detonation of an atomic bomb, sending waves of invisible destruction in all directions.

The swarm of living fear disintegrated, and there was nothing left but me.

With no time to think about it, I stared ahead and kept flying. I was almost there, maybe only two or three miles. The shapes of the individual Stompers within the two clouds were discernible now, and they looked like the essence of evil. Their shadowy, wispy shapes flew toward each other, all heading for the same point between them. I could just make out a tiny dark object there, floating in the air.

My eyes focused in on that spot, and I headed straight for it.

From the left and right, the Stomper clouds converged like two vicious storms meeting in the middle of the ocean. Closer and closer they got to the object from both sides. I flew on, willing myself to go faster. Like collapsing canyon walls, the gap between the Stompers grew more and more narrow. They were only a few hundred yards apart, and I knew that I wasn't that close.

At the current rate, I wasn't going to make it.

My body was weak, every last ounce of strength gone. That last push of the Power to get rid of the swarming nightmares had taken everything out of me. I couldn't feel anything—my whole body was numb. My brain begged to shut down, my spirits and energy spent to their last penny. *How?* I asked myself, with only a minute left until it was all over. *How am I going to do this?*

The Stompers were almost there. I could see it now—the object. It was a dark, crumpled bag—the kind you would take to the gym with a change of clothes. It floated in the air, waiting for the victor. A bag, representing the entire future of millions of people, hovering in the air, so close.

The two walls of the Stompers stretched out in the middle until two distinct points jetted out from the rest, heading for the floating bag. They were seconds away now.

I reached down, to somewhere deeper within than ever before, to a place I didn't know existed, to a place that defined what it meant to be human. I grabbed hold of the Power, and unleashed it to the fullest.

My body exploded forward with a loud boom. The power of it sent shock waves behind me that sucked dirt and rocks from the ground far below and thrust them into the air in a long trailing stream of dust. In those fractions of a second, time seemed to slow to the point where I could see everything around me develop as if I watched a movie in slow motion. As I rocketed toward the floating bag, to the soul of the world, I saw the first ghostly hands of the Stompers extend out from their formless shapes, reaching for the bag. Their misty fingers touched it, tracing along its edges, ready to fold up their hands and grab it once and for all.

But it was not going to happen.

In a blur of movement, I whipped past, the shock of my speed blowing the Stompers away with a violent rush of air. As I passed by, defying all known laws of physics, and not caring, I reached out, grabbed the bag by its handle, clutched it to my chest, and flew away to safety.

In that moment, I finally and truly saved the world.

CHAPTER 70

In the Bag

I landed with a soft bump miles away on a flat plain of dirt. Every last muscle in my body was drained and my every part ached. I lay on my back, looking at the blue sky, all signs of taints or clouds gone. There was also no sign of Stompers or nightmares. My hand still gripped the duffel bag.

With a groan I forced myself to sit up and I pulled the bag into my lap. It was very light and loose, like there was nothing in it at all. It was hard to lift my other arm—it felt like I'd been lifting weights for three days straight. But I managed, and I pulled the zipper that ran down the length of the bag.

I stuck my hand in, rummaging around for anything I could find. But the whole thing was empty—nothing. I pulled the two sides apart from the zipper and looked inside. *What the heck is this,* I thought. *This empty bag symbolizes the soul of an entire world?* We had a pretty pathetic planet if that were the case.

But then I saw a folded piece of paper within one of the creases of the bag. I reached down, grabbed it, pulled it out, and unfolded it.

It was a picture of my family.

Even as I caught the first glimpse of Rusty's red hair, Dad's fat belly, and Mom's big smile, the world around me started to spin, and I fell backward into blackness.

As something took me away from that place of nightmares, at first I felt confused. *Why a picture of my family?*

But then, I understood.

I woke up, flat on my back, looking at the same people I'd just seen in the picture.

"He's awake!" yelled Rusty.

Dad tried to pull me up but quit when I let out a big groan. "Are you okay, son?" he asked.

"Yeah, my whole body hurts, though. Where's Raspy?"

"He disappeared a long time ago. Joseph, come over here and help me get this guy on the couch."

Dad grabbed my arms, and Joseph my legs. A few sharp pains later, I was lying comfortably on the sofa. Everyone stood around me, now. Tanaka and Miyoko, Rayna and the Hooded One. My family. Joseph.

And the Half.

"We did it, bro," he said, and shook my hand. "That was some freaky stuff, huh?"

"You don't know the *half* of it," I replied.

"Boy, you're hilarious," he said back with a smile.

"I know. So . . . what happened? Is everything back to normal?"

"What *happened?*" Joseph said in a sarcastic voice. "I think you're the one who needs to tell us." As he spoke, I realized that we had to be inside the Yumeka still. We were in my uncle's house, in the same place where I'd entered the Black Coma—for the second time, I now knew. I was back in the First Layer, and so we still had waking up in the real world to look forward to. Or dread.

"My head hurts too much," I said, rubbing my temples. "I'll tell you more later, but basically I found out we've been living inside the Yumeka for a year. Then I went through a bunch of horror movies and grabbed a duffel bag to save the world."

Blank faces looked back at me.

"Can I have something to eat? Then I'll tell you everything." All of them ran for the kitchen.

It took me an hour, but I told them the whole story from beginning to end—choking up when I described how my family's picture represented the soul of my world. The hardest part to explain was the stuff about the Layers, and how we were still inside the Yumeka. How we still had one more time to wake up before it would truly be over. Mom cried a few times, and Rusty kept saying how cool it sounded. I was glad he saw it that way, at least.

Joseph and the other members of the Alliance kept looking away or dropping their eyes like they were ashamed of something. It didn't take me long to realize why.

"You guys knew about this, didn't you? That we'd been captured by the Stompers all this time?"

"Yes, we knew," said Rayna. "Of course we did. The Givers told us everything long ago."

"Me, too," said Joseph. "Sorry, kid."

"But what about all those stories of when you guys were taken into the Blackness?" I asked. "And that guy in Japan—that Ainu guy—that was the first one to enter the Blackness from this world. How does that work?"

"It's understanding the Yumeka," said Miyoko. "We all took our turn entering there. You just have to get past the fact that it was in our minds. That's true but only partly. The Yumeka is as real . . ."

"Yeah, I've heard that a thousand times," I interrupted. "You know what—forget it. I'm sick of thinking about it. We won. That's all that matters."

There we were, all the people I cared about, all of my family and friends, all together in happiness and safety, all inside what I hoped would be the last nightmare we ever had. The relief of it being over finally outweighed the constant confusion I'd felt since Farmer told me the truth.

But I should've known better than to expect such a perfect ending to my tale.

To my right, in the middle of the living room, a Rip in the Black Curtain appeared, its usual sound filling the room. We stared as two people emerged, holding hands.

It was Farmer and the little girl from under the Door in the woods.

It was time for everything to turn upside down one last time.

CHAPTER 71

Topsy-Turvy

"Hello, Jimmy Fincher," the girl said, her voice like ringing crystal.

"Uh . . . hi," I said, scrambling to sit up straighter. "I haven't seen you in a long time." I looked at Farmer. "What are you guys doing here? I thought . . ." I didn't know really what I thought. But it just seemed wrong that they were here. Before, I'd only seen them through the doors or inside the Stompers' realm.

"There's a very important reason we're here," said Farmer. "We have a lot to talk about."

"Why? I know we still need to wake up in the real world. What else are you going to pull on me?"

"Don't worry, you've saved your world, Jimmy. The Stompers are gone, back through the Black Curtain. The Shadow Ka, too. People are waking up all over your planet, already beginning to put their lives back together."

"Then what's the problem?"

Farmer sighed, and sat back onto thin air—his magical chair.

"Jimmy," he said. "I've dreaded this part from the very beginning."

"Dreaded what?"

A frown like I'd never seen creased Farmer's face.

"Asking you to never go home again. At least not for a very long time."

Farmer took a deep breath and leaned forward, resting his elbows on his knees.

"This is going to be hard for you, Fincher family. But please hear me out, and don't interrupt. Agreed?"

Mom and Dad nodded, and Rusty did nothing. "Get on with it," I said, dreading what he was about to say.

Farmer's eyes watered as he looked at each member of my family. Then he focused on me.

"Jimmy, it's time for your family to wake up and get on with building their lives again. But we need you to come with us back into the Blackness."

"What?" my mom and dad asked at the same time.

"Yes," Farmer said. "Yours is not the only world that needs saving."

The next few moments were filled with tension. My mom and dad were furious, and Farmer was left defending his request.

"He is part of a greater plan," he said, pleading. "The Four Gifts can never be repeated. Especially the Fourth, the Power. If Jimmy does not come with us and help us free the others one by one—they will live the rest of their lives in the living nightmares that you know all too well."

"There is no way . . ." Mom started again. Arguments blew up all around, but my mind focused in on what Farmer was asking. He wanted me to stay with him and help free other worlds from the nightmares of the Stompers. He wanted me to leave my real body asleep while I traveled with him back into the Blackness. He was asking me to sacrifice everything, fully and truly. And yet, I knew he was right.

"Please, listen," Farmer pleaded, raising his hands to stop the arguments. Everyone quieted to hear him out. "This is your choice—his choice. I am only asking. No, I am begging. Even if it's only for your world's sake, you must do this. If they are not conquered and eliminated, they will only figure out another way to come back. They don't stop. They never stop. They will do anything to grow and survive."

"But . . ." started Dad, and then everything exploded into arguments again.

"Stop." I stood, my muscles aching. "Mom, Dad—I have to do this." My mind was made up—not because it was easy or I thought I was some great hero. But I had just witnessed the full and terrible reaches of the Stompers. How could I live the rest of my life knowing that I hadn't at least tried to save others? It was the right choice—the only choice.

"Jimmy," Rusty said, "you can't do this!"

"No . . . no." I held my hands up, shaking my head. "I'll never understand this whole Yumeka thing, but I know that everything I've learned in this life is in thanks to my mom and dad." I looked at them. "After all that you've taught me, how could I *not* do this?"

There was more arguing, more pleading, more discussion, more tears.

But the decision was final. Instead of returning to my body, sleeping somewhere in the real world, I was going back into the Blackness to fight the Stompers.

Over and over again.

CHAPTER 72

Good-bye

A lot of things made more sense now. Joseph getting the money to buy the yacht, Tanaka's swim in the ocean, the *okisaru*—all of them were manipulations of the Yumeka. The Stompers weren't the only ones who could do it—they were just the most powerful. The Givers had their greatest influence in the Blackness itself, which explained its healing power and the cleansing magic of the inky water there—which meant almost certain death to the Shadow Ka.

I tried to get Farmer to explain the nature of the Givers, but he told me that was a tale for another day. We'd had enough mind-blowing details for a while. He said it was enough for me to know that they were the opposite force to the evil of the Stompers, which was just how things worked in the universe. I didn't push the matter.

Farmer also instructed me to use the last chance of the Anything to give myself complete control of the Black Curtain. He'd always said I would need one use of it in the end, and I was glad I had waited. The Curtain now would open and close only according to my command, and in that way Earth could be protected forever. It also meant that maybe I could come back someday. Maybe.

And so it was that I found myself standing in front of a Ripping to the Black Curtain, ready to do the hardest thing possible for a human being.

I had to say good-bye to my family.

I decided to start with Joseph and the Alliance and then save my family for last.

Joseph squeezed the breath out of me and then tousled my hair.

"I wish I could go with you, bud," he said. "But your family is going to need a lot of help. I figure that's the best thing I can do."

"Go with me?" I asked, incredulous. "What are you, an idiot? I'd never let you do that. Take care of them, all right? Baka, too."

"On my life, little guy. On my life."

I turned toward Rayna, but she stopped me before I got close enough to hug her.

"We *are* going with you," said Rayna. "The Alliance is going with you."

"What . . ."

"No, Jimmy-san," said Tanaka. "Don't try to stop us. We go with you. No other choice."

Miyoko nodded, as did Half, and Hood banged the Bender Ring against the floor. Even the ghost was going with me.

Something filled my heart, and the road ahead seemed a little more bearable. The thought of not going alone had never crossed my mind until that moment, but for some reason it made sense.

"Okay," I said. "If you're all dumb enough to do that, then I'll be glad to have you." I turned to Farmer. "But what about our bodies? Who'll take care of them?"

"Don't worry, son," Dad said, his voice trembling with emotion. "The whole world will be in your debt. I'm sure the full disposal of every government will be at your service. Joseph, Rusty, and I will make sure you're all found and taken care of. I promise."

"That's right, Jimmy," Rusty said. His voice shook too, and it meant the world to me. "Nobody's gonna come near your body until they get past me. Here, I grabbed this for you to take. For good luck."

He handed me the wrinkled, yellowed Braves hat.

I wrapped my arms around him. Mom and Dad joined us, and we stood there for several minutes, hugging and crying. When you love someone so much—when your whole life is defined by the care and concern for that person, there's no need for words. My heart and mind went through a whole range of emotions as we stood there together. I couldn't help but realize the irony of how this very thing had saved my family many times because of the Shield, and now it would be the last thing I did before saying good-bye.

"Jimmy," Farmer said, "it's time. Your family needs to get back and make sure your body and the others are safe from harm."

I started to let go, and Mom grabbed me, gripping me to her with all of her strength.

"I'll be there, son," she said through her sobs. "Every day, every hour. I'll be there, taking care of you, right by your side.

Remember that when times grow dark. I love you, Jimmy. I love you so much."

"I love you too, Mom." I was barely able to get the words out.

And with that, I had enough to keep me alive for years to come.

There were more hugs, more tears, and more promises. But we all knew it had to end, and it was time to go. Me, to the Blackness; them, to waking up in the real world.

Farmer and the girl went first, disappearing through the Rip. Then Tanaka, the birdcage full of *okisaru* in his hands, followed by Hood and Rayna. Miyoko and Half came to me, touched my arm, and I turned to go with them. They went through, and I looked back at my family one last time. With my eyes flooded by tears, I waved, and did my best to smile so they would remember me that way.

Gripping my hat, I stepped through the Black Curtain and sealed it shut behind me.

The battle for Earth was over.

But for me, the war was only beginning.

Epilogue

The little girl held the rose with one hand and her daddy's finger with the other.

He'd been talking all week about how it was time for her to learn something very important, and that they would be taking a special trip on Saturday. Last night, she'd been so excited that she could hardly go to sleep—almost like Christmas Eve.

But not in a million years had she expected this.

First of all, they'd been stuck in a traffic jam for hours, cars lined up before and behind them for miles, inching along like a snail with a sprained ankle. Just as many cars came from the direction they were heading—although not so slowly. At one point, a man in a uniform stopped their car and looked around it and under it with a flashlight. Then he looked in the trunk. He let them continue on with a wave, giving her a big smile. After what seemed like forever, her daddy finally pulled into a parking space and then helped her out of the car.

They stood in a line and then were let through a big gate with lots of sharp pointy things all over it, and followed a bunch of other people down a long paved road. Flowers were lying everywhere, and a lot of people coming from up ahead back toward them were crying.

Then she saw it.

Up ahead, rising above the crowd, was a huge pyramid-looking thing. Big steps went up and up and up until they got to a big glass dome. It reminded her of one of those Christmas thingamajiggers with water in them that you shake to make it look like its snowing inside. Above it in the sky, two helicopters flew in circles, with men sitting inside holding guns. She finally asked her dad what in the world was going on.

"All these men and women in uniform are here to protect something very special," he said. "Don't worry, I'm going to tell you all about it when we get up there, okay?"

"Okay, Daddy."

They waited in line for a long time again but finally got to the bottom of the pyramid. One by one, they walked up the steps, slowly following the people in front of them. As the glass dome got closer, it got bigger and bigger. She couldn't believe it could be so huge. And now she couldn't wait to see what was inside.

Finally, finally, they got to the top. A lady in uniform looked them over again, smiled, and then nodded toward the glass. All she could see now was a big wall of it since they were so close—it didn't look like a dome anymore. Her dad squeezed her hand, and they stepped up so they could see inside.

There wasn't much. A few nurses walking around, some machines, and other stuff that looked like something you would see when you went to the doctor. But what really caught her attention was the thing in the middle.

There was a big block of stone—a few feet tall, and pretty long. On top of it was a body—a man—lying on his back, with a pillow under his head and a blanket covering his legs. A tube went into his mouth, and she could just barely see his chest going up and down while he breathed. It should've given her the creeps, but for some reason it made her feel very warm inside. She laid the rose on top of some others on the ground.

"Who *is* that, Daddy?" she asked, looking up.

"He's the one who saved the world, sweetheart. He sacrificed everything to save me and you and Grandpa and Grandma and everyone you know. And now he's out there, somewhere, saving other people. There were others who went to help him—the Alliance—but their bodies are somewhere else." He paused for a long time, a blank look on his face. Then he nodded toward the man lying on the bed. "Anyway, a lot of people call him The Boy Who Sleeps, although he's not really a boy anymore, is he?"

"What's his name?" she asked.

"His name? Well, Miyoko, I'll tell you. His name is Jimmy Fincher."

Her dad's eyes got watery—something the little girl had never seen happen to him before. He rubbed her head like he always did and then looked down at her through his tears.

"And you wanna know the coolest part?"

"What?" she asked.

"He's my brother."

"Really?"

"Yep, he sure is. Don't you see your grandma in there?"

Miyoko looked closer, and sure enough, Grandma was sitting next to the bed, holding Jimmy's hand.

"Later," her dad said, "we'll go inside, too. I wanted you

to see it from out here the first time, to show you how special he is. Come on, I'll tell you everything while we walk back."

He squeezed her hand again, and she waved at The Boy Who Sleeps. Then they turned and started back down the stairs. Her dad began the story.

"It started with a tree . . ."

About the Author

James Dashner was born and raised in Georgia. Although he currently resides in Utah, he will always be a southerner at heart.

After high school, James attended Brigham Young University, where he went on to receive a master's degree in accounting. He also took a couple of years off and served a mission in Japan. Since graduation, he has received his CPA, worked for a major audit firm, and now works as a financial analyst.

He is married and has three children.

For more information on James and The Jimmy Fincher Saga, visit www.jamesdashner.com or email him at author@ jamesdashner.com.

About the Illustrator

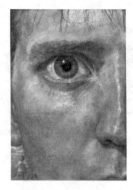

Michael Phipps grew up spending hours with friends drawing, imagining other worlds, making odd recordings, and building marble chutes and forts. He always knew he would be an artist as an adult, and he graduated with a bachelor of fine arts degree in illustration from the University of Utah. He loves to spend time with his family and friends, be outdoors, and listen to strange music. His art can be viewed at www.michael-phipps.net. E-mail him at art@michaelphipps.net.

0 26575 78796 2